ACCLAIM FOR MARK SLOUKA'S

lost lake

MARK SLOUKA

lost lake

Mark Slouka's story "The Woodcarver's Tale" won
a National Magazine Award in Fiction for *Harper's*
in 1995. He is a graduate of Columbia University
and has taught at Harvard and the University of
California at San Diego. He currently teaches at
Columbia and lives in New York City with his
wife and children.

lost lake

lost lake

STORIES BY

MARK SLOUKA

VINTAGE CONTEMPORARIES
Vintage Books
A Division of Random House, Inc.
New York

The Library of Congress has cataloged the Knopf edition as follows:
Slouka, Mark.
Lost Lake / by Mark Slouka.
p. cm.
ISBN 0-375-40215-2 – ISBN 987-0-375-70208-2 (pbk.)
1. New York (State)—Social life and customs—Fiction.
2. Czech Americans—New York (State)—Fiction.
3. Immigrants—New York (State)—Fiction. I. Title.
PS3569.L697L67 1998
813'.54—dc21 97-49471 CIP

Book design by Anthea Lingeman

w w w . v i n t a g e b o o k s . c o m

Printed in the United States of America

With special thanks to Colin Harrison, Sloan Harris, and Jordan Pavlin, who understood both tale and teller.

For my wife, Leslie, my son, Zack, and my daughter,
Maya, with whom I'm never lost

And for my parents, Zdenek and Olga Slouka,
who long ago cast the lines I tend

contents

lost lake

the shape of water

Some say the soul tempered by fire—tortured true—is
the better for the trial. Perhaps it is so. But I was born
between the wars. My adventures were of the surviv-
able kind, my tragedies ambiguous and undramatic,
observed as much as felt. What formed me were
anecdotes—often inconclusive, generally unheroic—
connected to a particular forty acres of water. An unex-
ceptional place. I did not choose it. And yet, if I could
ever open myself, I suspect I'd find its coves there, its
sleeping silt, its placental water smooth with algae . . .
and the faces of those I'd known, revealed as clearly as

if mine had been that lake of legend said to reflect the hidden heart.

I. Dream

I don't remember much: a small yellow fire burning on a flat rock, spongy ground that leaked warm as pee into my sneakers, a crushed circle of cattails, an old kerosene lantern throwing huge shadows out over the lake . . . I remember other men, shapes, appearing by the shoreline, then gone; my father sitting hunched on an overturned bucket; the huge night crowding in on our little circle and the lake glass-black and still and hardly like water at all. I remember the way sky met sky at the opposite shore, and I remember being afraid of that near horizon—windowless, blank, unmoored in a night of troubling doubled stars.

And I remember my father dragging a huge fish smelling of mud and vegetable rot up into the lamp-light. It had scales like silver dollars and a round, ugly mouth that kept kissing at the air and I remember watching it flop heavily in the crushed reeds, leaping in and out of the shadows like a thing accustomed to the earth, thumping the damp grass. But most of all I remember my father down on the ground struggling to take out the hook, holding the great glancing body pinned under the space between his knee and foot, its head flat with his right hand, working with the thumb and forefinger of his left—and the hook not coming out. I remember the broad bend of his back beneath his shirt, the rolled sleeves, the shine of sweat in the dark hair on his arms. He held the flashlight in his mouth, trying to see where the hook had bitten into the dark red gills, raspy and stiff as combs, his hand starting to shake from the strain, and then suddenly he looked up—he was turned half around from me—and I saw the beam leap up over the reeds and disappear into the sky as he let his hands find their own way around steel and flesh and then the barb was free and he had the fish in his arms like a child and had slipped it into the water and the water closed over it like a door.

When we shone the light down, there was nothing there—just the beam disappearing in green water as into some bottomless well and tiny motes of dust, myriad and fine.

Years later, when I asked my father about this, he didn't remember. He said he'd never gone fishing for carp at night as far as he knew, and this much was true, he'd never cared for fishing much, and anyway, who would the other men be? And where would the carp come from? Our lake had never had carp in it, and no one had heard of any being caught there. And even if he *had* caught a carp that size, why would he let it go? My parents were Czech immigrants. My mother had been making carp fillets and carp-roe soup for as long as I could remember. Another lake? We hadn't spent time on any other lake when I was that young—three, four at most—and the few relatives my parents might have let me go night fishing with weren't due to emigrate for another five years. And there were no cattails on the lake we knew and no extended shore without, on any given night, at least one lamp in a window to break the darkness.

II. *Loss*

I'm not sure when I first knew about the bottles behind the green half-curtain my mother had hung under the kitchen counter to hide the garbage can. Or when I first knew they were important. I used to go look at them sometimes when nobody was home. My favorite was a clean glass bottle with a red cap and a red label with a picture of a man on an old-fashioned sleigh pulled by huge black horses. He had red cheeks and a heavy beard and was dressed in a black bristly coat that looked like it had just come off a bear. There were great pines bent with snow and it made me think of Christmas.

It was around this time that the yelling started and my father slammed the door one night and the ceramic Indian by my window fell and broke off a part of his headdress. In the fall I slept under a hill of blankets in a small wooden room like a cave or a den, and when I woke up I could tell it was morning by the jays and the light coming through the two cracks in the wallboard by the door. Sometimes I could see my breath. My father would usually be up by then, and I could hear him slowly crunching the newspaper into loose balls and then the snap and spit of the wood catching and the good, sharp smell of smoke, and I'd leap out of bed and run to the big wicker chair where my pants and shirt and socks were already warming in the heat. He slept alone on the old gray couch by the wall. It had soft worn lumps like the hair on an old poodle. The cushions would be stacked on the table and I'd sit down on the sheets to pull on my socks and sometimes they'd still be warm from when he'd gotten up. The couch was a little short. I never realized the wooden chest— shoved flush against the couch—was anything more than a lamp stand.

"Mama still sleeping?" I'd ask.

"You're up early," he'd say from the kitchen. "Why don't you put a sweatshirt on."

But that's not what this is about. This is about the time my father went fishing. I was about eight years old then. I spent a lot of my time elsewhere. A while before dusk my father would walk out on our dock and whistle me in for dinner. He had a good whistle and I could hear him all the way out at the dam. When I heard my mother call instead I got scared. As I ran down the small catch-root path below the orchard I could see the boat was gone. I thought first somebody had taken it or it had floated loose and he was out looking for it. But I knew that wasn't it.

"Come and eat your dinner," my mother said, already walking into the cabin.

"Where's Dad?"

"He's gone fishing," she said.

We could see him as we ate dinner, sitting out on the empty float, the boat off the corner, drifting in half circles like a tethered horse. The float was maybe twelve feet square, a painted wood frame with a four-step ladder wired to eight empty oil drums and anchored to the bottom by a cable. As kids we played hide-and-seek between the drums, diving under to catch each other's legs, splashing water on the spiders that built their webs in the barred gloom beneath the boards. In the summer I'd lie on the hot wood and cup an eye to a crack and watch the bluegill drift up out of the cool green, disappear to the side, then drift back to view, hovering by the barrels.

It scared me to have him sitting out there with the sky turning dark and the insects starting up in the trees. My father could fix things and a friend had talked him into going bow hunting once when I was young, but mostly he sat at the table or up in the shack that used to be the old ham radio station, typing. He'd never gone fishing, never wanted to, hardly ever talked to me about it. With one exception.

It was over dinner. I'd been going on about a bass I'd lost in the cove. "You want to catch something worthwhile, you go out in the deep water," he said suddenly, sounding almost angry. He pointed with his fork. "It may be boring but you sit it out unless you want to piss around all your life." My mother had started to argue, in Czech, saying what was the difference, he should let me do what I wanted, it was ridiculous, and what did he know about fishing anyway. I didn't say anything.

He picked up his plate. "Fine," he said, as though I'd been saying something. "Suit yourself."

Just before dark my father sunk a hook into something that snapped the old surf-casting rod he'd found in the shed into a deep C. I saw the tip plunge under water, jerk up, then plunge again. He stood up, fumbling awkwardly at the reel. I saw him glance around as though looking for help, then his arms jerked forward and he started walking, grudgingly following whatever it was he'd hooked down there as it circled the float. My mother stood up suddenly as though to go outside, then slowly sat down again. I stared out into the near dark, watching him do everything wrong, forcing it, holding the butt of the rod jammed to his stomach like a curved spear—so that from a distance it looked as though he were struggling to wrench himself free of this thing, to pull it out of his body—fighting for every foot of line hissing off into the water like it was his birthright, wanting it desperately now when five minutes earlier he'd neither wanted nor expected much of anything at all.

It took almost twenty minutes. He must have had it close, because I saw him drop to one knee and, shifting the rod to his left hand, start reaching for the line. When the hooks finally straightened and the rod snapped straight to the dark sky he lurched back, then dropped to the other knee. For a moment he didn't move at all. When he put out his hands and fell on all fours like a man kicked in the stomach about to vomit, my mother got up quickly and walked to the kitchen. I went out into the dark. It took a few seconds for my eyes to adjust. He was sitting up now, perfectly still, the boat still floating obediently on its leash.

I didn't want to say anything. I sat on the end of the dock watching the bats, knowing he couldn't see me against the shore. At some point his voice came over the water and it was like he was sitting right next to me. "Go to sleep, kid," he said. "It's late."

He sat out all that night as the boat swung half the clock face in a slow pendulum and back, watching the shore, finally falling asleep on the cool boards, perhaps peering down like a boy into the dark heart of that lake, hoping to glimpse whatever it was that had escaped him.

III. Love

Odwin—I never knew his full name, or whether Odwin was his first or last name—was suddenly just there. I don't remember him coming to the lake and I don't remember him leaving. One day there he was in the gray rowboat, anchored in the middle of the cove in a cold June rain, and it seemed to me he'd always been there—I just hadn't noticed him. And then one day the cove was empty and the boat half swamped with rain-water and rotting in the muck, still tied with a rope at the bow to a post of the wooden dock, but by then it seemed like years since he'd left and I found I didn't remember much about him at all.

He was married then, to a blonde girl with a pale, pretty face, considerably younger than himself. He'd never held a rod before that afternoon at the Kleins' when, out of sheer politeness, he asked the old man about the spinning rod standing in the corner by the door. He held it the wrong way, with the reel sticking up into the air instead of hanging down below. Klein showed him how to hold it, how to catch the monofila-ment on the tip of his index finger—not letting it slip into the crease at the joint—how to flip the bail with his left hand, how to cast overhead and side-arm, releasing the line at just the right moment.

Odwin tried everything, opening and closing the

bail, reeling the small, silver-bladed spinner up to the top guide, then letting it fall to the ground, his glass in its little wicker holder on the table next to him, while the three of them, growing restless, began to talk of other things, then drifted back to the kitchen for more drinks, finally returning to the living room filled with the sound of rain on the windows and barred with strange watery shadows moving up the furniture and across the walls. Odwin stood there with the rod. He had an odd, soft smile on his face. He seemed mildly surprised.

"Where could I buy one of these?" he said.

By the next afternoon, Odwin was on the lake. Rumor had it he didn't row in until well after midnight. From that day on he was unrelenting—twelve, four-teen, sixteen hours a day. In two weeks he was an expert. Rain meant nothing to him. If he was sick, we'd hear him hacking out on the water and then at some point he wouldn't be sick anymore. He bought spin-ning reels, spin-casting reels, bait-casting reels and rods to match, dozens of spools of monofilament of various test strengths for different conditions. And lures—hundreds and hundreds of lures. Jitterbugs and Hula-Hoppers with multicolored skirts, Rebels and spinners and Daredevil Spoons, Bottom-Bumpers and Flatfish and plastic worms in every color of the rain-bow. He'd fill up one big-belly six-drawer tackle box and start another. And everything would be treated well: every reel lubed and smooth, every knot snugged, every point on every treble hook honed and perfect.

I don't remember much of any of this. I was only four and a half when he arrived on the lake. All I know I heard from someone else. And all I remember of Odwin is an impossibly tall man with black hair and a long, sad, bony face. But I remember some things. I remember watching him pull up to his dock early one evening. At night he'd bring a portable toilet with him. While there was daylight, though, he'd have to row in. I watched him pull in after eight or ten hours on the water, and when he tried to stand up his body remained in a sitting position. It took him some time to get out of that boat. He had to crawl out on his hands and knees. Once out of the boat he slowly laid out his entire length on the boards. He lay like that for a few minutes, staring up at the sky, then started going about the business of standing up. That's all I remember.

His wife left in the middle of the second summer. At ten in the morning she put two suitcases into the car and drove away, but not before she'd taken every lure out of every tackle box and thrown them off the front porch into the trees. There were lures everywhere, gaudy and sharp, some in the ferns, some up in the white birches by the wall, others hanging festively off the pine. Great blue-gray nests of monofilament littered the living room, the kitchen, rolled like ghostly tumbleweeds over the stones and under the potted plants . . . Odwin was out on the boat. He didn't come in until late that afternoon. By then he was the only one on the lake who didn't know.

Everybody watched him pull up, throw the noose over the middle post, hoist himself painfully out of the boat. By dusk he was back on the dock. We could barely make him out. It must have been June because there were fireflies and he stood there for what seemed like a long time and I remember swallows flicking down around his head and you could smell the rain. The lamp in the Bauer cabin went on, making a yellow trail on the water. It ran a few feet out from Odwin's dock like a path. You could see the water all pocked and busy, but it wasn't rain yet, only gnats and mayflies and the lapping rings of fish sipping off the surface. I don't remember seeing him get into the boat, but suddenly the pale rectangle of the dock was empty and undisturbed and the dark bulk of the boat was gone and there was just the steady creak and thump of a loose oarlock bumping against the wood.

There was much talk about all this, and Odwin wasn't a strong man, or a ruthless one. My father was the only one who'd speak to him still, and even he did it not for Odwin, not out of love or respect or mercy, but because no one else would, which to my father had always seemed like a fine reason for doing anything. So no one was surprised when Odwin barely lasted out the season, packed his things and left. Certain kinds of love can only stand so much resistance.

And Odwin was the greatest of lovers in his own sad way. It wasn't obsession that kept him out on that boat as the moon rose and set and the stars wheeled on their axis like a slowing merry-go-round. It was love. On a small road after dark one night (a grown man now), I heard voices on a wide porch and thought for a moment they were speaking in the language I hadn't heard since long before my father died. I was wrong, it was just a trick of the breeze or the night, but in those few seconds before I realized my mistake my breath had caught in my chest and tears had gushed to my eyes and I felt like a child stumbling up the final steps to home. I understood Odwin then, though I could never know the particular deserts he'd traveled, the specific thirst he hadn't even known he was enduring until, like some mad Bedouin wandering the empty quarter, he stumbled upon the thing he'd forgotten he'd been searching for and in that moment lost not his mind but his heart.

The bend of reed, the shallow bulge of water, the tucked ecstasy of damselflies linked on his sleeve—these things and a thousand like them he loved. The rods, the reels, the lures—these were just the paraphernalia of courtship. He fished the way suitors of old would play cribbage or gin rummy, not because they cared for cards but because it was their ticket into the sanctum, into the presence of their intended. Like them he could hardly bring himself to pay attention to the game, and, also like them, he couldn't seem to lose. The lake offered up its prizes to him, and he happily dragged them home.

Two fish—extravagant, absurd—stand out from all the others. The first was a bass twenty-three inches long with a big potbelly and a mouth twice the size of a man's fist, this out of a lake where anything over fifteen inches would magically attract small knots of boys who would hover nearby, whispering and pointing, and who wouldn't leave until the fish (gutted, cleaned, and wrapped) had disappeared into the freezer.

But the other was unforgettable. My father woke me early one morning to see it. "You don't want to miss this," he said. "Odwin's dragged up something special." It was laid out on the stones of the veranda when we got there, a gleaming yellow-green beast fully half the length of an oar. I was six and a half that summer. I'd never seen a pickerel before. I remember there was moss and little tufts of grass growing between the rocks. My father walked out back to look for Odwin.

It was getting hot. I stared at the canary-yellow diamonds on its sides, the sharp white teeth in the partly open mouth still locked on the diving-minnow lure he'd caught it on, the way the colors faded into the dark-olive back . . . I remember the yellow jacket that settled

on its long, bill-like snout and moved down the jaw,
tentatively touching the cartilage flap of the mouth, the
teeth, then the dark-green cheek plate near the eye.
The fish didn't move. I stood away. There was something horrible about this: the delicate, strangled body,
the venomous yellow abdomen twitching spastically,
edging toward that great staring eye. I half expected the
fish to start thrashing at any moment and I remember
I thought of walking away, and even started to, but
the wasp was already at the rim of that clouding
pool. And I saw its forelegs dip down—gently, almost
respectfully—and it was like a swimmer testing familiar water, or an acolyte paying homage at some long-
forgotten shrine.

IV. Fear

They moved into the cabin up the hill in midsummer,
the year I turned twelve. One day we heard a man
laugh and then a woman squealing, "Put me down, you
bastard, I swear I'll kill you, I'll . . . ," and we saw him
walk out on the dock holding on to her legs and her
beating on his back with her fists, and then he grabbed
his hat, turned once, and flung her fully clothed and
furious into the water. "Looks like neighbors," my
father said. From that moment on the lake adjusted to a
new topography. My world circled around them like a
plate on a pin.

It was particularly hot that summer, or maybe I just remember it that way. Every morning the cicadas would ratchet up and by breakfast the sky would start to whine and all day a thin head of clouds would build to the west but nothing ever happened. Even swimming didn't help—the top three feet were as warm as the air. We'd dive down into the olive dusk, cold as mud, and hug the boulders of the old pasture wall to keep from floating up, but that only made the surface and the overheated air still worse. Sitting on the boat I'd listen to the birds fighting in the locked maples over the road. I was like the blackwater pockets in the spillway by the dam—choking, crazy with life.

On a boat one afternoon with the water stamped flat and hot, I pulled in a small bass with a minnow still sticking out of its throat. I tugged on the minnow's tail and it slipped out of the creamy vortex of guts as easily as a cooked almond slides out of its skin. All afternoon I'd been dunking my head over the stern. And suddenly I did something I didn't know I was going to do: I put the tip of my finger where the minnow had been, to see what it was like. The inside of the fish's throat was smooth as vanilla pudding, and when I pushed deeper it started to swallow at me with quick, hard draws and I jerked my hand out quick and threw that bass out over the water so hard it skipped. It seemed everything was like that. I hardly knew what I'd do next. I was quick to anger, quick to tears, an utter mystery to myself.

Things would change in ways I didn't expect. Cleaning fish, for example. I'd been doing it since I was seven. I'd hold them in an old pink towel with just their head sticking out and give them a good whack with a smooth, bent iron, then put the tip of the knife into the vent and cut up through the belly to the gills. The knife would make a soft, ropy sound and the white skin would collapse a bit like a man pulling in his cheeks, and if you lifted up a side you could see the guts all connected. The heart was right up front, tucked under the gills: small, dull red, easy to pop. It reminded me of the thin little bubbles we used to suck and twist out of the tatters of burst balloons. Back behind the liver was the stomach, sort of a mud-colored bag: inside you could sometimes find whole minnows, crawfish . . . once I found a small frog turned creamy white and another time a fake gold earring. I never went near the gall bladder. I'd cut it once by accident, and it leaked thick and yellow and smelled like old men's pee and reminded me of that time at the city train station a man had stood next to me looking straight up at the ceiling like there was some message written there and all the time shaking his wrinkled cock like an old dog wags its tail.

Against the vaulted roof of the spine was a dove-gray bladder you could poke with your finger. I'd always liked doing this but that summer for some reason I started trying not to. I'd make little bets with myself,

imagining rewards, picturing horrors if I didn't stop.
Usually I'd do it anyway. It wouldn't hiss or pop but
only tear thin and sweet, and I'd wash the meat clean
under the outside faucet, picking out the little bits of
blood with my fingers. It was that way with everything,
more or less.

There were three of them, the oldest hardly twenty-
two, polite and somehow dangerous, and it surprised
no one when the state police appeared on the dirt road
and pulled into their drive, only that they left soon
afterward, taking no one with them. There was one
who'd call out to me sometimes when I rowed by. He'd
be sitting up on the stone porch with his boots up on
the rail wearing only a pair of pants and a big broad hat
with a turned rim, and he'd ask me how the fishing was
or where I thought he'd have the best luck, and sometimes somebody else would say something from inside
and he'd say, "Why don't you shut up, Tucker," without
even turning around, and I'd row away, repeating the
words he'd said and the way he'd said them, flattered
that he'd talk to me at all. Sometimes I'd see her leaning in the dark of the doorway, eating something off a
paper plate with her hands, then licking her fingers.
It was always hot, and sometimes she'd turn half
away and lift the hair off the back of her neck with her
forearms.

Every night as lightning flashed like some rapid code above the horizon of trees they'd be out on the boat, setting a trotline from the end of their dock to a branch hanging over the water. The next morning one of them would lift the line with a grunt, and there, dangling on the end of a dozen small drop lines, would be foot-long bullheads, black-speckled crappies, sometimes a bass or a small snapping turtle. Then somebody would go out and pull hand over hand along the line, cutting the fish into the boat with a pair of scissors, dumping the rest over the side. I'd never seen a trotline before.

"Hell, easy," said the one who talked to me. "Come on by and I'll show you how to skin a catfish."

The sky had been rumbling since noon, and where the path left the uncut meadow and entered the trees it was like dusk. It was hot, and when I slapped at the gnats and deerflies that circled around my face they stuck to my skin and hair and I had to pick them loose with my fingers. They were all sitting on the porch when I got there. Music was coming from inside and I could see him already working on the fish, straddling a bench with a cleaning board nailed to it crossways, the fish jammed headfirst in a bucket of water by his side.

She was lying in a hammock strung between a hook in the cabin wall and another sunk into the tree at the corner of the porch, wearing only a long skirt and a man's sleeveless T-shirt, and I could see the sweat on her arms and her throat and the damp curve of her breathing. The hammock was barely moving. She'd pulled up her skirt to get some air, and one raised knee tipped outward slightly, then closed with each swing of the pendulum. Her arm, hanging loose over the side, trailed slowly over the rocks. She'd been facing my way when I appeared by the side of the cabin. She didn't say anything—if her eyes had been closed I'd have thought she was sleeping—and after a few moments simply turned her head the other way. One of the men got up and walked into the cabin. No one else said anything either.

He must have known I was there all along. "Well, come over here, boss," he said, without turning around. "You ever see this before?" I could see sweaty curls of black hair sticking out from under his hat. Reaching into the bucket, he pulled out a foot-long bullhead, laid it belly-down on the board, and quickly poked a small hole in the top of its skull with the tip of the fillet knife, then, reaching up to the railing, picked up what looked like a wheat straw and slipped it into the hole. Suddenly I felt myself swallowing high up in my throat like I was going to be sick. The tail trembled with current. He moved the straw, delicately, as though mixing a small drink, and the fish shuddered again and was still. "See that?" he said.

A man's voice said something from the house and I could hear her laugh behind me. "Why don't you give your little friend a drink, Troy?" Her voice was like her fingers tracing over the rocks. Again the other said something I couldn't make out. She turned to the house. "Maybe I will, asshole. At least he'd know what to do with it."

I couldn't move. I couldn't say anything. I was suddenly just scared. I could see the lake, still and dark as oil, but everything looked different from here—the tilting, unfamiliar dock, the float on its barrels, too close to the cove, like the cables had snapped or the anchor broken loose. Through a space in the leaves I could see my father walk out on our dock, and it was as though I were seeing him from another world. I willed him to stay. I watched him light a cigarette with quick, familiar movements. After a while he turned and walked back, disappearing. A fish swirled tight by the shore.

"You make a cut here," the man said, and I watched him slice in a half circle behind the gills and again at the base of the tail and four more lengthwise and then, grabbing a small flap with a pair of pliers, peel the brown skin down like you would a banana, baring the clean white meat underneath. Two quick moves and the whiskered head, spine, and tail dropped on an open newspaper. He reached for another. I wanted to run.

I don't know how long I stood there, trapped by things I didn't know: the spotted blade, the blood-marked straw, the pliers going about their business, and at my back the gently creaking mesh, the small sounds of exhaustion—a long sigh, a stretching yawn.

———

I knew he was there before I heard the hammock move behind me. "Hello," she said, startled.

I turned around. "I thought I might find you here," he said quietly, looking at me. "If you're hungry, it's time for dinner."

We went back up the hill and into the light of the meadow, neither of us saying anything. Here and there I could see the lake through the trees, rearranging itself. A flash of light cracked low on the horizon and a few fat drops hit the tall grasses, making them jerk and nod in the still air.

"Come on, let's run," said my father.

V. Truth

And then there was the water at the dam that spilled over the boards in their iron sleeves and down around the rocks and small islands with whippy three-foot saplings doomed to a season, maybe two, before the next big rain in May or June ripped them loose and sent them floating like pruned branches in the current.

This was small water: a short, undercut bank, a thigh-deep hole along a toppled tree still partly rooted, its branches now growing vertically like trees in their own right but still feeding off that troubling, recumbent soil. No one over twelve would notice it. Where the spillway flattened out and ran under the one-lane wooden bridge, it slowed to a stream less than five strides across. The bridge was so low you couldn't stand up, and when cars rumbled over, sand and small pebbles would hiss into the water and the boards would groan and you'd wonder if *this* was the time they'd give and crack and the steel belly of some car would come crushing down into the wet, dark place you were hiding in. That stream was crammed full of fish (trapped by the dam on one end and a long, sandy shoal on the other) that had been carried over the spillway as fingerlings: bluegill and pumpkinseed and redear, the occasional bullhead or perch or small bass. The shadows were ridged and thick with their backs, and they'd churn across the shallows in great, nervous schools. We'd chase them back and forth for hours with our nets, herding them like sheep into the dead ends under the rocks and banks and back under the bridge against the base of the spillway, trying to see how many we could get to a scoop.

It had been raining for a week and now it had stopped, though everything still ran water and the clouds scraped low and heavy over the hills. The lake was brown, the trees along the shore a foot deep in water. I went down to the stream to see what it was like, carrying a long-handled salmon net I used for snapping turtles on the open lake. It had a two-inch mesh, much too big for anything I might find there, but I'd torn the netting on my other one so I took it with me anyway.

I could hear the water long before I got to the bridge, bigger now, bulging up over the fallen tree and rushing in a straight gray line through the woods. The water looked barren—scoured smooth and dead. I sat on the bridge for a while, watching broken half tunnels of bark and leafy branches appear from under the wood and disappear downstream, and then, having nothing better to do, got up to walk along the bank. Fifty yards down I recognized a small, sink-sized pool, relatively unchanged, and stuck the handle in to test the strength of the current.

A tail wide as a dinner plate slapped the water and disappeared. I stared as though a large pig had stuck its snout above the surface, snorted, and vanished. It was simply impossible. This was a bluegill hole hardly bigger than a kitchen pot. A fish that large would have to be curled like a doughnut to fit at all.

At ten the eyes still occasionally win over the mind; I spun the net like a baton, stabbed it into the hole (so narrow the rim just made it), and, leaning in, forked a huge fish with big silver scales out onto the bank. It promptly flopped out of the mesh. I tackled it, literally wrestled it flat. I probably screamed when it finned me in the stomach (it must have hurt, and I flaunted the neat row of small black puncture holes like a certificate of honor for weeks), but I don't remember.

I *do* remember leaving the net behind and dragging it by the gills (which also cut me fairly well, as I discov-

ered later) almost half a mile back down the grassy
middle of the road as it started to rain again and the fish
revived every few minutes just enough to thrash loose
and leap across the dirt and into the roadside weeds.
Pictures were taken. No one had ever seen a carp
around there before. It measured thirty-four inches by
the yellow cloth tape my mother kept in her sewing kit,
the one in the circular case with the button that sucked
it all back in when you pressed it. My mother wanted to
keep the fish for soup, but it would have been a big job
and it was raining and the fish still alive, its plate-size
gills working hard, so we picked it up and hauled it to
the end of the dock and threw it like a log into the
water. It lay stunned just beneath the hissing rain, then
churned into the dark. "Be a lonely life," my father said.
"Nothing like him in *this* puddle, that's for goddamn
sure."

It had probably come up from the river with the big
rain, he'd said. It would be years before I'd remember a
circle of lamplight stamped from the darkness, a horizon dark as dream, my father dragging a fish with scales
like silver dollars into the sudden air—years before I'd
be old enough to believe that life, like water, will sometimes engineer its own logic, adjust itself to fit the form
of our desires.

genesis

It began with the lake, I suppose, long before I was born. By 1914 it was already a sanctuary, a forty-acre stillwater pond created not by god on the fourth or fifth or any other day, but by a one-armed veteran of the Spanish-American War named Simon Colby, an impassioned fisherman who, local legend had it, could drop a plug into your pocket at thirty yards without your ever knowing it, his fat, work-callused thumb feathering the drum of that level-wind reel as gently as a father touches the hair on his child's head. Growing tired of his daily four-mile walk to Wall Pond and the domestic arguments it inspired, Colby, not untypically, decided to build his own.

A tall, rangy man with tobacco-stained fingers and a walnut-sized Adam's apple always bobbing the length of his neck like an agitated cork, Simon Colby had early on acquired something of a reputation throughout rural Hutchinson County as an intemperate man, a man whose life seemed to be forever careening from crisis to crisis. "Like a level on a horse's ass," proclaimed old Herman Washburn, who even then seemed given to the kind of country aphorisms doomed to pass into TV and myth. "Always thirty degrees off plumb."

A fighter, a lover, a man of enormous industry when inspired and biblical laziness when not, Colby, Washburn claimed, returned from the war late January 1899. Leaning back on his three-legged stool early one morning in 1951, Washburn explained the chronology of Colby's return, at length and in detail, to my father, who, like everyone else visiting Washburn's store, could only wait patiently while his goods, hostage for the length of the telling, gathered dust on the plywood counter.

"Now here's the thing, Mostiky," said Washburn, who, having never quite succeeded in getting his tongue around our Czech surname, Mostovsky, had simply whittled it down to size. "Bein' from Europe and all, you probably never heard of the Spanish-American War." My father, who should have known better, started to point out that he had, in fact, heard about it, that he'd read about it in books, of which Europe still contained a few, and that . . .

"Anyway, we had us a war with the Spanish," continued old Washburn, "short as it was. Now here's the thing. Colby goes down in March, you see." (And here Washburn raised the thumb of his right hand, knobbed with age, and bent it back with his left index finger, counting.) "Shafter's boys kick the Spaniards' ass in July." (Right index finger.) "Santiago falls on the seventeenth." (Ring finger.) "But Colby"—and now the right hand, unbound, rose briefly as though releasing a dove, the gesture unintentionally graceful, a mixture of wonder and alcohol-inspired exaggeration—"Colby doesn't get back till the following January. What took him so long?"

Here Washburn, pausing for emphasis, finally brought a delicate, silver flask from behind the counter and raised it to his withered lips. "Well may you ask," he said, grandly. Then, leaning forward: "Sonofabitch walked. Said he didn't like the company so he got off the train in Macon. Half a year later, there he is, walkin' up the Croton Road through a January blizzard. Now of course Jack's is empty on account of everyone bein' at the dance, so he has a drink or two by himself, then walks two miles straight to the barn, out on the dance floor, grabs . . . Look behind the rakes for Chrissake! . . . grabs Mandy Sullivan 'round the waist as she's dancin' with her beau at that time, man name of Frank White, god rest his donkey soul, and kisses her full on the lips right then and there in front of everybody.

"Now, far as anybody can figure out afterwards, Colby's never seen the girl before; her family come to town while he was gone to war. No, she just happened to be the finest-lookin' woman there—damn near any-where, you ask me—and the nearest one to the door when he comes stompin' in, black hair fallin' in his face, and grabs her without even bothering to knock the snow off his coat. It would've all passed in fun (and I still say that's how Colby meant it), if the Sullivan girl had just seemed a little more shocked by it—if she'd pushed him away or smacked him or *any* goddamned thing—or if poor old Frank had only laughed and taken it all in stride."

Here Washburn, holding forth from behind the counter, looked over the small line of customers wait-ing patiently like acolytes at the temple gate, and sadly shook his head. "Trouble is, you see, Frank White never took anything in stride a day in his life. A big man—all hair and muscle and not much else. I've talked to peo-ple say they saw him smile, but I don't believe it. Always looked like he had a plug up his ass to me.

"So anyway, they go outside in the snow, White in his shirtsleeves, Colby still wearing his boot-length army-issue coat. White takes a pose like Great John L. the day my daddy saw him go seventy-five rounds at Rickburg—he has fists like this—and tells Colby he can apologize or eat shit. Colby laughs in his face, says: 'Look here, Franklin, here's what I'm gonna do. First, I'm gonna kick your ass with one arm behind my back. And then'—it seemed to come to him at the spur of the moment—'then I'm gonna marry your girl.' Whereupon he steps in, lets loose a haymaker with his left—and misses. White, meanwhile, unleashes one of those hams of his and damn near takes Colby's head off. This goes on until someone stops to wonder why Colby's right sleeve keeps flapping like a shirt on a line, but by this time he's not much to look at. White, the last to know he's been beatin' on a cripple, rushes over to where Colby's tryin' to get up after paintin' the snow with his face. He starts to blubber and apologize, but there's Colby, lyin' on his back, lookin' up quietly into the falling snow. There's a little bubble of snot goin' in and out at his nose and he's workin' his mouth like he's huntin' for something with his tongue. 'Get your suit, Franklin,' he says, spittin' out a tooth. 'You can be my best man.' "

Leaning forward once more, Washburn took another sip from the flask, for all the world like some huge, bald-headed bee at a wavering blossom. "Now you're probably wonderin' why I'm tellin' you all this. I mention it, Mostiky, to give you some sense of Simon Colby. A mind like a C-clamp. Decided he'd walk from Georgia to New York just for the hell of it? He done it.

Decided he was gonna marry this girl in spite of the fact he couldn't pick her out of a crowd of three and her with a two-armed boyfriend twice his size—a month later by god they're married. And remember this— building that lake of yours meant a whole lot more to Simon Colby than walkin' from Macon or marryin' Mandy Sullivan ever did."

We knew the rest of the story, of course. Everybody did. Summoning his older brother, John, one fine summer afternoon five years after his return from the war, Simon Colby supposedly led the way up the grassy rise already known as Cobb Hill. Below them lay a gently undulating meadow abruptly pinched off at one end by the rising hills. Thirty white-spotted Herefords, comprising the brothers' modest herd, grazed as though spellbound in the slanting light along Polson Brook; one, having crossed the water, lurched awkwardly onto the undercut bank, heaving up its oddly human buttocks. A few, seemingly deep in thought along the pasture wall, seemed to have forgotten their purpose.

Simon Colby, blind to the bucolic splendor of it all, looked on the scene with mild disgust. John, god-fearing and sullen, annoyed at being dragged away from his work in the barn, said nothing, determined to wait his younger brother out. Minutes passed. A woodpecker hammered in the afternoon silence. A cow, chewing its cud patiently, turned to look at the men on the hill. At long last, having searched for words and found none, Simon scratched his stump with his left hand, sighed, and delivered himself of a line destined to go down in Lost Lake history. Years after he himself would be buried on Cobb Hill, only a few yards from where he now stood, it would be repeated as a miracle of succinctness and resolution. "Better get your cows, John," he said.

A man of vision, Simon Colby was constructing the first of twenty-three rough wooden cabins before the waters of Polson Brook had begun to shove against the boards of the new dam. The stones for the foundations he acquired by dismantling, over a period of twelve years, a full half mile of pasture wall, which he loaded and hauled over broken field and hardpack with the help of a very young Herman Washburn and, most particularly, young Washburn's horse and cart. Living out of an old U.S. Army tent (his decision to sell off half the family herd and flood the pasture for a fishing hole apparently having gone over badly at home), he had the first stone rectangle in place before the remaining Herefords, clustered head to head on a soggy rise as though plotting revenge, fully realized the permanence of their situation. By the time the grass had disappeared forever under the waters, Colby and Washburn had raised the walls, built the chimney, finished the roof, and shingled it. By October Colby had rented the finished product to a city man named Winston Reed for the unheard-of sum of one hundred dollars a year. A few days later, Simon Colby folded up his tent and returned home, a vindicated (and forgiven) man.

Some eleven years later, on a cool, sun-shot day in June, Simon Colby, Herman Washburn, and a nineteen-year-old Italian immigrant named Ludovico Mazzola finished the twenty-third (and last) cabin, and rested. Sitting on the spine of the roof, passing a celebratory bottle, Colby looked over his domain, to the stone chimneys rising here and there among the trees, to the cove where a lone swimmer, like some pale fish gasping for oxygen, slowly made his way, and declared himself satisfied. "Well, *that's* done," he said. Young Mazzola, who had the slightly wild good looks and guileless charm of a faun, and who forever seemed to be marveling at his own good fortune, murmured a benediction in Italian. Washburn drank.

The date was June 28. The year, 1914. I like to think of them sitting there, as in a photograph never taken, utterly unaware of the forces about to be unleashed on the world—unaware, like weary sunbathers drowsing in the sun, of the wall of cloud rising quickly from the east. What were they doing, at the precise moment the bullet left the barrel of Gavrilo Princip's gun? What were they thinking as the crowd, voices rising and ebbing with the summer wind, milled along the sun-warmed cobbles, unaware that in the coming instant the curtain of civilization, like a moving background caught on a nail, would be torn down the middle?

Herman Washburn, it seems, was thinking about nothing more essential than getting the bottle back from Simon Colby. Colby, tentatively probing an aching molar with his tongue, was thinking about a bass he'd lost the night before. Ludovico Mazzola, sitting slightly lower down the slope of the roof, meditatively sucking a cut on his hand, was recalling with no small wonder the night before at the children's dock, where—suddenly, unexpectedly—he'd had the Greenwoods' oldest daughter, Polly.

The morning wore on. The sun crossed an open patch between the leaves. The whiskey descended the neck of the bottle, then the waist, dispersing its warmth through the arms and legs of the three men who one after the other rose and walked down the sloping shingles away from the lake to piss off the side of the roof. Around noon, Mazzola climbed carefully down the stone chimney and tossed up a small leather sack with sandwiches to Washburn, who missed, lunged, and nearly followed them over the side, to the great hilarity of all concerned, himself included.

Had anyone been listening that morning, they would have heard a conversation whose margins kept getting wider, a conversation, that is, with the trajectory of a happy life, or a child's descent into sleep: at first, three voices, often overlapping, punctuated by bursts of laughter; then long, satisfied pauses, a sentence here and there, an occasional belch; finally (except for a brief, halfhearted argument over a hammer), a long, luxurious slide into silence and slumber.

Those still looking for signs of god's benevolence (or proof of his disgust) need look no further than our ignorance of where our lives will lead. Ludovico Mazzola, tasting his own coppery blood in the sun, couldn't know that he was fated to spill the rest of it into the plowed fields of the Argonne only four years later, or that the woman he'd had the night before would become his wife, delivering some nine months later the child they'd conceived (despite her assurances about the prophylactic properties of water) the night before, or that that child, an uninspired student and second-rate carpenter, would inherit some of his father's early good fortune and open a small hunting and fishing store on a rural dirt road literally weeks before the powers that be in Albany would decide to turn it into an interstate artery, thereby bringing in a steady supply of commuters and cash and boosting the Mazzola family fortunes for generations to come.

Colby and Washburn, for their part, could not have guessed that they'd outlive their smiling apprentice by nearly half a century, or that Washburn's love for the bottle would remain the one true passion of a long and garrulous life, or that Colby, some thirty years later, would first rent a cabin to a Czech immigrant named Rheinhold Černý, and then another, some months later, to another, younger émigré from Czechoslovakia named Mostovsky—my father.

Innocent enough in conception—a forty-acre fishing hole with a float like a wooden rivet at its center— Colby's lake was the start of something, of many things, he could never have anticipated. Like a water hole on the savanna, like the original garden, bloodless and pure, it soon drew unexpected guests, and in this it was typical of all the things men dream and do. Dismantling one wall, he erected another; flooding one world, he exposed a dozen more. It could not have been otherwise.

portrait—a sketch

He'd start out every evening just after dinner, moving the heavy wooden boat slowly east along the shoreline with a single oar he pulled out of the oarlock and moved in small, effortless circles with his left arm, locked and strong. I'd never seen a fly fisherman before. I'd watch the line loop the air in a long, tight script, the rod curved with its weight, his right arm lifting it sharp behind his head, letting it rise and stretch, then sending it out to the open spots between carpets of weed, the black pockets between deadfalls, the rectangles of shade under sagging docks.

He was old—seventy, maybe more—tall and straight, with gray hair cut close to his head and a face that always seemed to be listening to something difficult to make out but not unexpected. Everything about him— the patient set of his mouth, his eyes, the way he'd put down the oar and loop the line between the thumb and little finger of his left hand—was slow and deliberate and perfect and in such complete and incontrovertible contrast to the frenzied chaos of tangled lines and snagged lures that marked my hours on the water that I watched him as if mesmerized, sensing something special and mysterious, determined to learn whatever secret there was to know.

"Hey, mister, what're you using for bait," I'd say with the callow familiarity of youth, automatically using the generic term we had for anything tied to the end of a line. And he'd always answer the same way: "I'm not using bait, son, I'm using a lure." He'd show me a little homemade popper with a spooned-out face and dry fly hackle tied around the shank of the hook. He seemed to have five or six of these and nothing else. I never saw him change lures. I never saw him fish with anything else.

It didn't matter to me that a good part of the time he didn't catch a thing. It certainly didn't seem to matter to him. On good days he'd put two fish on a simple rope stringer he'd hang from the steel brace below the oar-lock. If he caught more, he'd let them go, slipping out the single hook, holding them gently upright under the water till the lactic acid wore off and the gills started to pump and they swam slowly off his hand, then flashed into the dark. He kept nothing under a foot long, nothing much bigger.

I was there the time he dropped the floating lure beside a small finger of branch sticking out over the surface. The instant it smacked down like some fat, wind-spun moth, the water beneath and around it shifted almost imperceptibly. He twitched it and the water boiled briefly and was still. I watched from thirty feet away—we had just passed. He waited, until I thought for sure whatever it was had gone, then twitched it again and the lure disappeared in a great splash and his rod was bent deep to the water. He brought it to the boat, slowly, carefully, a great, thrashing slab of a fish that broke the water only once, wallowed heavily, then went deep. I watched him slip the hook, as he did with all the others. He held it up for my benefit.

"He's huge," I said, barely breathing.

"A good fish," he agreed. "A pretty fish." He laid it belly-down on his palm in the water. It lay fanning quietly, then swam off.

It didn't take long for me to start despising my heavy fiberglass rods and the bulky reels and the arsenal of treble-hooked lures, each in their little compartment in the tackle box I lugged on and off the boat each day like some water-bound traveling salesman. I begged a cheap fiberglass fly rod for Christmas and by May I was back, whipping at the water, flinging mad loops around my ears, wrenching at the rod to loosen the poppers I invariably sank into the branches of lakeside trees just beyond my reach . . . By June I'd given up, returning to my Mitchell reel and the old familiar lures. That fall I started high school. I didn't pick up a fly rod again until after our first son was born.

He and his wife didn't come back to the lake that summer, or any other. Summer rentals were like that sometimes. It was years before I thought I understood the rough poetry of the man, the expression on his face when he looked across that small water—mildly amused, almost wry—as though to say, "It's not quite the way I planned it, not quite where I thought I'd be, but good enough, it'll do . . ." and began to suspect that living appropriately sometimes requires a drawing back, a slow renunciation of much that mattered, once.

feather and bone

I was three, no more, when I spotted for the first time the paleness of his shirt moving like some small, disembodied ghost against the darkening trees. Even now, the image remains, fixed in the scent of moldering wood: a man standing on a stone porch at dusk, his left hand crossed below his chest, smoking a pipe. It's June. Unaware of us approaching through the darkness under the trees, he stares ahead into the gathering night as though the past itself were inscribed there, as though the dip and weave of swallows in the last light were scrolling his fate in the disembodied air. From the path below, holding my father's hand, I see him above us. Fireflies rise around him in slow, languid gusts like sparks from some missing fire.

It's been nearly twenty years now since I last saw Rheinhold Černý, since my feet, barefoot or sneakered, negotiated the footpath to the cabin on the hill. From where it left the hardpack to where it opened into the meadow, that path was as familiar to me as my own mother's face. I could have run it blind, stutter-stepping through the marshy grass, swinging wide around the poison ivy, hitting the plank over the brook—right, left, right—then up and over the boulder with its little opaque windows of mica before leaping the strange, jointed root on the second turn past the shed . . . as though my feet, hitting earth and stone and wood, had stamped by some alchemy of correspondence each and every feature into the soil of my heart.

It would be Mrs. Černý I saw first, standing in the garden wearing an oddly formal dress and a wide straw hat, pulling blooms past their prime, loosening soil with a spade. She'd turn or straighten when I called from the bottom of the meadow, then walk up with me through the uncut grass into the chill shade of the cottage where she'd pour mint tea with honey and ply me with pieces of *jahodový táč*—strawberry tart—that left crisp flakes of pastry on my lips and chin. The cottage itself, always dark despite the cut flowers still blooming on the windowsills and tables, smelled of smoke and stone, wool blankets and sweet tobacco, and I'd linger happily, dangling my feet off the rough oak bench by the dining-room table. We didn't talk and didn't need to. I'd sit and eat and she'd busy herself in the living room or the kitchen, coring a piece of fruit or sweeping the crumbs off the counter into an open palm with quick, expert movements I found strangely reassuring. Nearly sixty at the time, she still carried about her an old-world sense of style and reserve, of unthinking diplomacy and tact.

We both knew, of course, that it wasn't the honeyed tea or the *jahodový táč* that brought me dashing down the path every Saturday morning, and just about the time I'd begin to fidget and peer out the living-room window, she'd be standing by the back door, calling, *"Rheinholde, mladý Mostovský je tady"*—young Mostovsky is here—and soon after that I'd spot him (momentarily caught in the frame of the kitchen window like some forest spirit escaping its own portrait) walking through the knee-high bracken. Spare and tall, inescapably patrician in his grass-stained khakis and small, frameless glasses (despite the weeds caught in the straps of his sandals and the dirt caked on his hands), he'd first wash his arms to the elbows in the basin by the door, then carefully brush the dry dirt off his soles with a few strokes of a stiff-combed brush that hung from a nail above the bench. Only when these things were done would he look in.

"Vítáme vás," he'd say, never smiling despite the absurd formality of the greeting. "I see you've fortified yourself well for the rigors of the day. Truly a chip off the old block, eh?" he'd add to his wife. "His father, too, is always prepared." Mrs. Černý, answering from the kitchen, would mumble something inaudible, to which he'd chuckle, then beckon me through the doorway with a sweep of his arm like a coachman in a medieval fairy tale. *"Půjdeme?"* he'd ask. Shall we?

The teasing, mild enough and diluted still further by a very real affection, meant little to me then. If it ever made me uncomfortable, if I ever sensed a touch of condescension beneath the banter, I assume I accepted it as somehow justified, given my own family's flailings and failures, or ignored it by virtue of the mercenary single vision of childhood. Rheinhold Černý, you see, built or brought or showed me things, week in and week out, and for this, more than anything else, I loved him.

While my own father was off in the one-room shed that had once served as a ham radio station, typing on the old Underwood with the broken *e* and *c* keys, Černý was pointing to the blood-red crest of a woodpecker as long as my arm, pounding fist-sized holes in the side of a rotting oak, or showing me, through an opening he'd cut in the shoreline thickets, a pickerel and its shadow in the sunlit flat by the swamp. A luna moth, ghostly and pale, that he'd trapped against the screen at night, an old coffee tin with a half-dozen turtle eggs wrapped in moss, a barred feather, perfect and huge, that he'd found in the garden—every week it was something new.

The pain of returning to the city every Sunday night from September to June would be lessened, time and again, by the wonders in the trunk of the car or on the seat next to me, wonders a quiet six-year-old well down the first-grade pecking order could ride, like a pet panther, into the hearts of all the Sherrys and Susies and Samanthas for the short space of each week's show-and-tell, eclipsing utterly the urban Lotharios reduced to peddling their fathers' collections of watermarked three-cent stamps. Sometimes, indeed, my contributions required an advance call or two—as much for courtesy as clearance—to prepare teachers for, say, a small colony of paper wasps buzzing inside a gallon jar, or a milk snake in a box with a sliding glass lid, or an outraged baby heron—given to both fish puree delivered through a paper straw and to rhythmic and unremitting shrieking—standing one-legged at the bottom of a parrot cage.

Distracted by their own lives as they may have been, my parents were nonetheless quick to recognize the power and status these things conferred, and rarely stood in my way. Whatever their feelings for Černý (and

I was alert enough to pick up, even at that age, their growing resentment of the man—of his brusqueness, his patrician airs, his position in the émigré community), they couldn't help but appreciate (at least partly because they may have suspected, in their weaker moments, that Černý's condescension was not entirely unjustified) his kindness to me. In a world without grandfathers, Černý had, with a certain amount of rough grace, stepped into the role, and if relations with the middle generation were a bit strained, well, that was not unusual, even among real families. Our apartment on the fifteenth floor above Sixty-third Road in Queens soon took on a strangely animate cast—feathered, furred, and antlered—and my father, burying whatever jealousy he may have felt for my benefit, simply stepped, like a rejected suitor, back into the shadows. My mother, though temperamentally more cautious, less quick to concede, eventually followed suit.

They would have done well to pay attention. I can say this now, of course, because time, like an inverted telescope, shows clearly what was once too close, what proximity (and love) kept hid. Eye to the lens, fully thirty-five years and more since those summer afternoons I spent in his company, I see again the square-fingered strength of his hands, the veins in his pale wrists where they emerged from his shirt always rolled one button up, the way he would peel his rimless glasses from his face to wipe the sweat or grime with a clean handkerchief. I remember the comfort of his silence, his old-man's smell of tobacco and cologne, the nod of approval I'd receive for understanding something he'd shown me, or applying it well. The burst of tart on my lips, the smell of orange mushrooms (laid out to dry in the sun like battalions of finger-sized soldiers), the stench of the mud where the goldenbloom grew . . . all these I remember. All these I see.

But the landscape now reaches easily from sun to dark, skirting depths I never knew: Černý's descriptions—always precise, analytical—of nature's horrors; his chuckle on finding the oddly human head of the mantis he had kept for months in a tabletop cage (the cat had apparently moved the lid) staring up from the living-room carpet like some ghastly green mint. Or the particular look in his eyes—detachment, perhaps—that morning we watched a mud-dauber wasp, iridescent and thin, battling for its life in a spider web under the eave of the outhouse. Wrenching, thrashing, buzzing furiously, it tried to bring its abdomen around, but found itself bound in coil after coil of gossamer silk. Something about the drawn-out desperation of the thing moved me, I recall, and I thought of bringing a stick down through the web to set it free, but one glance at Černý put the thought from my mind. We watched the wasp disappear, bit by bit, leg by leg, until all that was left was the buzzing, and then even this grew muffled and the spider, straddling his trussed and broken feast, delivered the fatal sting.

I am aware, of course, that none of this troubled me then, that I felt nothing but love for this man—for his gruffness, his strength, his way with the world—and saw nothing but love returned. I am aware, too, of how easily the past is shaped by our fantasies and fears. I have heard, finally, those who say the past, like any distorting medium, like water, bends whatever enters it, and that the truth or lie of the broken oar is something we can never know.

I am reminded of all these things by a small, perfect skull, hardly larger than my first, which sits on a pile of books on my desk. Rheinhold Černý gave it to me two days before my seventh birthday, and I can remember still, with absolute clarity, the thrill of expectation rising in my chest as he led me by the hand to the compost heap and then—carefully, almost tenderly—began digging in the dirt with a small stick. I remember the bones growing up out of the soil, seeing for the first time the sockets of the maxilla, the rounded ball joint at the base, the perfect and beautiful ferocity of the canines. I remember the way he brushed it clean with an old toothbrush he took from his pocket, the way the skull fit the jaw like a lid on a well-made box—hinged and tight—and I remember him holding it up to me, in front of his face, and opening and closing its jaws in time with his own.

I look at it now (still held together by the wires he twisted himself that same afternoon almost forty years ago), and I say to those who claim the past is forever unknown to us, I have run my hand the length of the broken oar, and I know what is bent, and I know what is whole. Rheinhold Černý, almost smiling behind his rimless glasses, his hands, hinged at the wrist, dramatically opening and closing the jaws of that long-lost raccoon for the benefit of a little boy stunned with gratitude, is someone I loved like a father. This much is true. And this also is true: in his own particular way, he was a monster beyond reckoning.

It began, I suppose, the night my father turned the old DeSoto off the blacktop onto the rutted dirt road that ran around the lake. Already sleeping, my face pressed into the crease of the seat, I woke to the sound of the grass in the median swishing against the steel beneath me, and mentally began ticking off each familiar turn and lurch. Thinking I still slept, my parents were quiet. Every now and then I could hear them whisper to each other in the dark, a word or two each, no more.

"What's that in the road?" said my mother, suddenly.

"I don't know," said my father.

By the time he'd eased the car to a stop in the darkness and turned off the motor, I was up and staring bleary-eyed at what appeared to be a dog-sized stone or lump of mud set down at the end of the headlights' beam. Taking the flashlight from the glove compartment, my father turned off the headlights. It was as though the car around us had suddenly disappeared. Night was everywhere. Insects sawed back and forth in the trees, wild, arrhythmic, an army of elfin woodsmen. "Let's have a look," he said.

It wasn't until we were ten feet away that we realized the thing was a turtle, its huge, rocklike shell brown with age. It seemed a monster from some other world, accidentally caught in the land of families and electricity and cars. Leeches big as my father's thumb clung to its scales; its skin, loose and leathery, bulged around its head and legs. It struck at us as we came near, once, twice, hissing with each awkward lunge, then settled back, its gaping mouth pale in the flashlight's beam. The smell of mud rot and carrion rose in the air.

My father, squatting ten feet away with the flashlight in one hand and a crooked stick he'd picked off the road in the other, shook his head in wonder. *"Ty seš mně obluda"*—you are a monster—he said quietly to the turtle hunkered down in the dirt. Then, practicing his newly acquired English: "How are you? What's up?" The turtle hissed softly. "Fine, thanks," said my father. "Not much. And you?" He chuckled.

"Je pozdě, Pavle"—it's late, Paul—said my mother. "Stop tormenting the poor turtle with your English."

"Nothing like this back home, Marie," my father

said, and, squat-stepping forward a few feet, he waved
the stick in front of the snapper's jaws. *"Na toto jsme
emigrovali."* For this we emigrated. His words were
punctuated by a hissing lunge and the clack of jaws. A
foot-long piece of my father's stick lay in the dirt.

Rather than move the thing, we drove around it, I
recall, the car bumping and scraping up and over the
shoulder to the soft ground of the meadow, then back
onto the dirt. Looking back through the rear window, I
saw it sprout its Pleistocene head and clawed legs and
begin plodding, heavily, through the redness of the tail-
lights toward the still waters of the lake.

From that day forth, the snapper filled my child's
need for unseen things to fear; reeking, primitive, it
moved, always, somewhere below the surface, lending
that border a magic, a resonance, it might never have
had without it. Every swirl, every half-glimpsed shadow, every sensed or half-sensed thing moving in the
deep-green rooms cut by the shadows of trunk and
branch hinted at its presence; hinted, that is, until, on
some still afternoon, gentle as a Corot painting, an
angler in a rowboat, lulled into disbelief, would start at
the sudden apparition risen by his side: ungainly, ana-
chronistic, a griffin on a table.

I see him standing at the end of his dock at dusk, a
large salad bowl of crusted bread cradled in the crook

of his arm. With his free hand he tosses handfuls of
bread, like flakes of light, to a family of swans. They
duck and glide around him, wriggling their feathered
tails. One rises, flapping, its wings momentarily pinned
against the dark water. Getting down on one knee, like
a suitor proposing to his spell-locked love, Černý
reaches out. Though I can see little else, I see this
tableau, as though frozen in time: his body, balanced
and sure, the paleness of his extended arm, her neck
dipping gently down.

I remember the swans above all, but Černý's love
was hardly that selective. A practical, rational man for
all the years I knew him, he nonetheless had one weakness. No less than half a dozen feeders, some with
suet, some with seeds, surrounded his cottage; houses
for wrens and grosbeaks and woodpeckers, lovingly
built and situated, peeked from under eaves and
branches or nestled in the crotches of oaks. A pair of
ancient Zeiss binoculars, bulky and strong, were never
far from his reach, and his ear, like a trained musician's,
could pick out the slightest change in the twittering,
peeping ensemble performing round the clock, it sometimes seemed, for his benefit and his alone.

Calls, nesting habits, migration patterns and flight
characteristics, identifying marks both at rest and on
the wing (and all the possible variations thereof), all
these he had learned like the irregular verbs of some
dying language, until he was able not just to speak it,

but understand it, inhabit it. On certain spring mornings, I remember, I would find him standing with his eyes closed in some far corner of the garden, the expression on his hypnotized features—the slight, involuntary movements of his lips and eyes beneath their lids—suggesting a beatitude bordering on rapture. Feeling slightly awkward, I'd wait silently for the spell to pass. He always knew I was there. *"Poslouchej, Mostovský,"* he'd say quietly, his right hand raised like the hand of Adam to some ascendant god. *"Poslouchej."* Listen. *"To je krása." That* is beauty.

I wasn't there when it happened. I didn't see the swan, pushing eagerly through the shallows to Černý's dock, suddenly jar, then plunge like a child's cork beneath the surface. I didn't see the one wing tearing at the surface, or the boiling water, or the upward gush of bloody quills, rising out of the dark.

But I'd seen it before, and accepted it, somehow. During the course of every summer, fully half the ducklings would die, wrenched into oblivion as abruptly as though tapped by the hand of god. And every May, the survivors would be back, paddling the shallows, nesting in the reeds. Life seethed and sank and rose again. More profound than profligate, nature threw its endless battalions into the consuming fire, then drew them forth again. Everywhere it was the same: the frog, I knew, spasmodically kicking its way down the snake's expanding throat, had left strings of milky pearls in the shallows of the brook; the cottontail, still running in the talloned air, had fathered dozens . . . "Only waste is wrong," my father had told me once, and of all his lessons that faltered or failed, that one stayed true.

But Rheinhold Černý, standing in his rowboat, helplessly plunging a wooden oar into the watery dark where bits of down now seemed to jerk and swim like embers over an open fire, reckoned his world by some other, starker calculus: the creation, like a stuttering watch, had revealed its flaw, and had to be made right. Calmly, he presented his case: the turtles were ugly, served no discernible purpose, regularly killed the waterfowl whose beauty and grace was cherished by every local resident, young and old. He himself had seen them pull down a full-grown swan. Clearly it was time to reduce their numbers, to lend a shaping hand to a situation badly out of control. He himself would do the work, take care of all details. All he asked of his neighbors was their leave to do what, regretfully, needed to be done.

My father alone tried to protest the plan, to ask questions, though even he, frustrated as always by the older man's reasoned maturity, his air of seasoned wisdom, his perfectly calibrated condescension, soon found himself helpless. Sitting with my mother on the Černýs' stone porch one deep summer evening, yellow citronella lamps flickering and a Mozart aria playing from inside the cottage, my father, hunching forward in his wicker chair, tried to raise the subject. Why not wait to see if the depredations continued? he asked. Why not call some expert for advice? Or why not simply pick up a few of the nesting turtles and transport them to another lake?

Leaning back, one lean, trousered leg draped easily over the other, Černý picked a pouch of tobacco off the table, opened the sumptuous, black foil, and began to stuff his pipe. A single flick of his wrist and a match flared. Holding it to the bowl, he took two meditative puffs, each accompanied by a slight popping sound of the lips. *"Milý pane Mostovský"*—my dear Mr. Mostovsky, he said finally, his voice wearily descending the syllables like a parent lowering itself to speak to a particularly obtuse child—"the depradations have continued long enough. Experts can only confirm what we already know. And as for wandering about the countryside, hoping to stumble across a wayward turtle now and again, well, that is a solution that strikes me as singularly ineffectual. No, my dear sir"—and here I could see my mother gently place her hand on my father's arm—"what must be done must be done, and, as the Americans are fond of saying, a job worth doing is worth doing well."

"That would depend on the job," said my father quietly, his jaw set.

"Jak rozumíte"—suit yourself—said Černý, and then, to his wife: "What about that cake you've been promising us, my dear."

Ever competent, ever thorough, like a carpenter in his workshop, he gathered his tools: thirty plastic gallon jugs, carefully rinsed of milk or vinegar or carburetor fluid; forty yards of double-gauge wire, rolled off the wooden spool at Washburn's Store; fifty stainless-steel hooks, size 6/0, from the small saltwater-fishing section of Mazolla's Bait and Tackle.

Mazolla's son, Paul, just seventeen at the time, bagged the hooks for him. "Bluefish?" he asked, substituting, by the usual hunter's shorthand, the object of the quest for subject and verb and everything else.

"I beg your pardon?"

"You goin' for bluefish?" He pointed. "The hooks."

"Ah, yes. No." Then, after a pause: "Turtles, I'm afraid."

"Turtles?" asked Mazolla, uncomprehending. "What for?"

Černý accepted the bag and change. "Because, young man, they're a nuisance." The little brass bell over the door had already jangled his exit when Mazolla spoke again.

"That's a lot of turtles," he said, nodding toward the small paper sack.

Černý paused in the open door. "All of them," he said quietly.

But then, nothing happened. Those few who had given the matter any thought in the first place simply forgot about it, assuming, with some small relief, that Černý had quietly taken care of things in his own way, or abandoned the plan altogether. Labor Day came and went, bringing with it the return exodus to the city. By late September, the majority of cottages hidden behind the trees stood locked and silent.

My family was usually among the few who insisted on pushing the season, yet that year, hindered by my father's obligations in town, we came rarely. I remember long, hazy days spent playing on the city playgrounds or in vacant lots, the huge blocky shadows of the buildings advancing a strange silence across the heated asphalt, dulling, as though under water, the far drone of the freeway. I argued and cried, of course, for a last weekend, a last escape, before the long rain of November set in, but there was no help for it.

You can imagine my joy, then, and my parents' relief, when the Goldsteins, our neighbors at the lake, offered to pick me up one early Friday morning in mid-October, take me with them, and have me home in time for dinner. They were going, they said, to clean and lock up for the winter. I was welcome to come along. At six o'clock the next morning, I was waiting with my father in the first light along Sixty-third Road, holding only a lunch bag, a two-piece rod, and a tackle box into which my mother had slipped a change of socks.

The first thing I remember from that day is smoke rising straight as an exclamation point above the trees from the Černýs' cabin. The second is seeing something white burst above the water under the overhanging trees, disappear, then rise again a few yards down.

I had rowed quite close before I realized the thing was a plastic jug, wired like a huge cork to something under the surface. I tried to catch it with an oar, but each time I approached, the jug—as though alive, and not merely an indicator of something living below—would plow a panicked furrow under the surface, reappearing a few yards away. I chased it along the shoreline for a while, and then—I don't know why—instead of rowing on to the Černýs' dock, slid the rowboat into the reeds and set off on foot.

There were no omens, no premonitions. The garden was empty, the house strangely silent. Smoke like a quickly blurring ghost still issued from the stone chimney. I didn't call or hallo the cottage or the shed but instead walked around the house and into the woods as though following a string, straight to the top of a small, wooded rise.

Below me, inside a chicken-wire enclosure nailed to a circle of trees and carefully staked to the ground, was Rheinhold Černý, in hip boots and work gloves, moving about an old stone garden. A wheelbarrow lay on its side, its third wheel slowly spinning. To the left, by the fence, lay a pile of white plastic jugs, each connected to what appeared to be a fist-sized rock. I was about to call when a movement on the far end of the enclosure caught my attention. A stone was climbing the wire fence.

The mind runs slower than the eyes—it took me a moment to grasp what I saw. When I did, I vomited in the ferns.

Distracted by his work, Rheinhold Černý never noticed the little boy crouching like an animal in the bracken. To this day, if he lives, he lives unsuspecting that someone saw what he did that October day, that someone watched, like Dante over the ninth abyss, as he walked among the dying and the damned still dragging at the end of a yard-long wire the jugs by which he'd drawn them from the deep; how he pulled them to the wooden circle, one by one, their thick clawed legs scraping resistant furrows in the dirt; how he placed a foot on their useless shells, drew out their leathery necks by the wire still clamped to the hook in their throats, then severed their heads with two or three blows of a well-honed hatchet.

Even now I see them crawling, their reptilian hearts too stubborn or dull to die, past their own sudden heads (still twisting and snapping like ghastly roots wrenched from some dark and troubled soil), past the growing pile of jugs by the fence, past their own brothers, who might hiss, if able, or continue on, mute like themselves, to the fence, which last barrier they

would then begin to climb—unbelievably, absurdly—
as though the memory of freedom had somehow out-
lived both their comprehension of it and their need for
it, as though stopping their lives on the other side of a
chicken-wire fence were a matter of some importance.

Pausing in his work, Rheinhold Černý pushed up
his glasses with his shoulder (his right arm pointing
straight ahead as though indicating something in the
distance to an unseen companion), then walked to
the fence. Carefully removing one soaked glove with
the other, he hung them over the top wire like a pair of
small bodies, freshly killed, then reached for something
he'd left in the crotch of a tree. The lenses on his face
sparked, then died. I watched him reach into his shirt
pocket, then tilt his head in that familiar gesture I'd
come to know so well, but by then the branches were
already whipping at my face and I was flying headlong
from the petrified silence of that place (marred only by
the scrapings of claws on dirt) and the sight of Rheinhold Černý seated on an overturned bucket, one leg
draped over the other, enjoying a smoke before com-
pleting his work.

I said nothing, revealed nothing, quick, like most
children, to feel shamed by the shameful acts of others.
I removed that day from my memory like a photograph
from an album. The next season, I saw Černý again.
I smiled at his teasing, listened to his anecdotes,
accepted his gifts. And if, like any absent or invisible

thing, that emptiness ordered the world around it, if it affected my life in any way at all, it did it in the time-honored way of troubled ghosts and buried memories, by supplying action and effect without agent or cause, by rearranging the portraits and the furniture of my life in ways I could neither control nor fully understand. I developed a lifelong affinity for the silent and for-gotten, for those who couldn't scream. I swerved around snakes, stopped for tortoises, picked snails off rainy sidewalks. It was as though, forty years dead and buried, even the bone of their shells reduced to dust, the snappers still stumbled inside of me, as though their own indomitable blood were somehow my own, as though the compassion never shown to them had been passed, through the offices of my own shuttered heart, to all their kind.

Just so will evil sometimes undo itself, give birth to the sons and daughters who bury its fondest dreams.

the woodcarver's tale

My Father's Story

These are the facts as my father told them. In the old country during the Second World War, in the forests and villages of Czechoslovakia east of Brno, a man named Machár, or Macháč, made a name for himself as a smuggler, moving entire families across the Moravian border to Trenčín, then across Slovakia to Hungary, where others would take them on. His was the first and most dangerous leg in that human relay, a route as treacherous for its maze-work of forest paths as for the fields and towns and cemeteries that stitched the land-scape tight and close; windows were everywhere.

But Machár could do what others could not. He was the son of a *lesník*, an expert gamekeeper and woodsman. It was said that he knew the Moravian landscape—the forests of spruce and fir, the mustard fields folded into the hills—as no one else; that he would move through it, use it to his advantage, with the thoughtless surety of an animal. That in winter dark, with the bowled smoothness of the trail filled with snow, and no moon or stars, he could find his way by the changing shape of sky showing through the trees.

From time to time word would come back from those he had helped across. This was of no small importance. Refugees were easy prey: they brought everything. No one knew they were going. No one would know if they didn't arrive. And every spring, coatless, shoeless bodies, gold fillings wrenched from their mouths, would thaw out of snow banks all along the Hungarian border. Unlike some others, apparently, Machár would not steal or kill.

My father said he thought he might have met Machár himself in 1938, the spring before Munich. It was in Žďár. My father was stationed there, a member of the officers corps put in charge of organizing the local militias. Machár (if, in fact, it was Machár) was a powerful, not overtall, awkward man. A peasant, slightly stupid, instinctively suspicious. My father remembered him standing against the wall, sullen, generally unwilling, hands hidden in the baggy pockets of his gray canvas pants, giving not the slightest indication of hearing, much less understanding, anything being said. The only reason my father noticed him at all was that at that time Machár was already known in the region south of Hlínsko, in a small way, as something of a curiosity, an anatomical freak. Although the rest of his body was normally proportioned, his hands, apparently, were monstrous: not misshapen or hideous so much as simply outsized to the point of deformity. My father never saw them himself since the man by the wall never took his hands from his pockets.

But his hands alone would never have been enough to pull the man up from the floodplain of utter obscurity. Nor would his work as a smuggler have done so. Machár was an unlikely candidate for sainthood: gruff, uncommunicative, pathologically intense, frightening even to those he helped. The only reason anyone ever had cause to recall Machár at all was a story that surfaced toward the end of the war, in 1944. In January of that year, in a scene so unlikely, so ridiculously dramatic it had to be true, Machár, while leading a family with three small children at night through the forests south of Bošany, was surprised by two German soldiers on either side of the trail. One only had time to yell, *"Halt! Wer da?"* before Machár had seized them both around the neck, pressed his huge thumbs into the soft space beneath their chins, and snapped their spines like a pair of spring rabbits. He laid them in the snow along the trail, and the group continued on. A testament not to bravery but to outrageous brute strength, the explosive fuel of fear. In any case, it was enough. His name, for a short while, flickered in the great dark; then it, too, went out.

The war ended (quietly, ambiguously, like the fine breath of rot raised by a thaw) exactly on April 26, 1945. It wasn't much, my father said: no Soviet tanks bucking across the soaking fields, just one man on horseback, a Cossack, at dawn, watching only his own slow passing in the dark windows, riding slowly up Zejrova Street to the foot of the vineyards, then slowly back.

After him came others, two, three at a time. This was the liberation: no regiments, no heavy artillery. German snipers still held the hills outside Brno. At night they would pick off the silhouettes of the Soviet soldiers against the fires of boards and bench slats blazing in the road until some of the men, my grandfather among them, couldn't stand it anymore and went out and said for the love of god stay to the side, why die for no reason? And apparently, the story goes, one of them looked up from where he squatted by the flames, then out into the vague darkness my grandfather had indicated, then back to the fire. *Da nicego. Nas mnogo,"* he said. There are many of us. My grandfather had already crossed the street when the man spoke again, not looking up from the fire. "Hide your women, old man. We're not the last."

The *havět*, the vermin (General Malinovsky's troops), came later. *Špína*, my father called them, dirt, the after-scum of the general army: illiterate, ragged, undisciplined, many of them two and three years on the front. They moved through from the southeast, a bestial tide, monstrously unpredictable, unafraid to die. Some, like stunned children, were capable of small, absurd gestures of generosity. Some gobbled toothpaste, squeezing it on their bread like pâté. My grandfather, hearing the sound of breaking glass and the crash of piano keys, came downstairs to find one, pants pulled down around his ankles and rifle by his side, using the Austrian baby grand as a toilet. When he was done, he left. Some raped a ten-year-old girl. She died. Four months later, they were gone.

By the fall of 1945, President Beneš had returned from exile in London. By winter, the free press had returned to Czechoslovakia. And Machár was out of work. He went back, as far as anyone knew, to whatever it was he had been before the war. He disappeared.

The rest is almost too thin to tell: it offers no resistance, takes no shape. It slips through the sieve like water. Some remembered that Machár had worked in the *strojírna*, the factory, in Žďár. That he drank. That he had a foul temper. That he married a woman from Třebíč, and that the marriage for some reason had gone bad. Some recalled hearing about his father, a *lesník*, a gamekeeper, tortured and killed by poachers sometime after the first war.

A man from Javorník whom my father once met on a train claimed he had heard that Machár had escaped to Vienna after the Communist coup of 1948. Or maybe to Munich. That he had returned across the fences for his wife. And again for his child. That he had been seen in the refugee camps near Innsbruck in the winter of 1949, where intellectuals and journalists threw bricks to each other to roughen their hands and improve their chances of being farmed out for laborers' jobs in Australia and Brazil. That he had returned to Czechoslovakia years later. Alone. That he'd been living, a broken man, somewhere near Jíndrichův Hradec.

My father shrugged. Lives are such baggy things, he said. Sometimes there are pieces left over. He looked out the window, not seeing the snow, the trees, the burdened wires. That's all, he said.

But of course it's not. In death as in life we push against the universe of facts, force a space, elbow our way like pups to a teat. And the world adjusts. Eternity, such as it is, is in the echo. Our lives continue to sound long after we are gone.

My Story

Years before I had heard of Machár, sixteen years, to be exact, before that long winter afternoon when my father told me what he remembered of a man he had probably never met, a drunk in a green Trabant dropped me and a woman I had been living with at a crossroads not far from Telč, Czechoslovakia. It was a hot late afternoon in July of 1974. We were hitchhiking back to Brno and from there to Vyškov, to visit her parents. All day long she had been picking herbs along the wayside; they filled the huge shoulder bag she carried with her everywhere she went. She smelled like herbs. She was naked under her crumpled skirt and loose cotton sweater. She had fine golden fur on her legs and arms and stomach, and a small white scar on her left breast. We were both giddy with making love. Neither of us could remember eating anything and neither of us was hungry. I was not yet twenty-two years old.

With the sun still high in the poplars bordering the road, we started down a long hill thick with the smells of manure and cut hay and somewhere, coming from the village below, the fresh sweep of water. We seemed to unfold the season as we went. By the time we reached the bottom she was glad for the sweater. A fast, clattering stream ran behind the village along the base of a steep hill, then cut to the center and under the main road. We stood on the bridge and listened. Except for the water and the far bark of a dog, everything was quiet. In the little town of white houses with clay-colored roofs and small, cramped gardens, I soaked my head under a pump while she went into a store to ask directions. She came out with two bottles of sticky-sweet yellow *limonada*. We drank them sitting on the rim of the well. The last bus would be coming through in an hour. A few doors down, apparently, there was a woodcarver's studio. I cupped my hands and drank some water.

There was no sign. It took a while for him to open the door, a big man with a heavy drinker's face and small, close eyes. A growth of white chest hair, stark against his reddened skin, sprouted from his unbuttoned woolens. *"Ano?"* he said, stooping slightly forward under the door frame, one hand behind the half-opened door, the other propped behind the wall. She explained why we'd bothered him. He stared at her, mouth slightly open, rocking forward with each labored breath, until she started to say it again, then reached for a set of keys and shuffled past us down the walk.

A stone path, sunk into the earth and overgrown with weeds, ran along the house, then bisected a poor, shady garden with kohlrabi and radishes and a few ragged heads of lettuce. A chicken turned nervously on the gate of a wooden fence, then squawked to the ground. We passed through to a sort of thick-walled shed, plastered and rude, maybe five meters square. He unlocked the door, the key clinking minutely against the steel, then moved aside.

We stepped into a white plaster room with a small,

dusty window set deep and off-plumb, a cracked cement floor, rough pineboard shelves running the length of the walls from floor to ceiling. In the center, a hard-backed chair and a small table. The carvings, arrayed like infantry, lined the walls. Of the hundreds there, perhaps a dozen were of square-legged horses or face-less turtles or small, moored rowboats with pencil-thin oars. The rest were devils. Some were medieval, with straight, ropy hair and chiseled faces, sharp as an ax. Some were fat, grinning, tall as my forearm. There were small groups of miniatures, each the size of a man's thumb, with tiny horns the size of a grain of rice.

"Mě znají ve Vídni," he said suddenly from the door-way. They know me in Vienna. He stopped, standing away from the wall like a rooted tree, hands in his pockets. I nodded. Very nice, I lied. My friend nodded her agreement. This one's wonderful, she said, gently taking a small, naked devil off the shelf. The wood had dried badly. A small crack ran lengthwise from the nape of the neck, halfway down the back. He didn't say anything.

I brushed past her, pretending to be absorbed, and walked further along the wall, wondering how soon we could leave and whether we would have to buy some-thing. I could feel the way her sweater slipped easily over her skin. I wanted to be outside.

In the end we bought a carving and left. I'm not even sure who picked it. We missed the bus that afternoon and ended up walking away from the road, straight through patchy woods and briar tangles and across small streams thick with stinging *kopřiva* to a place by a deserted cow pond, where we made love on our clothes laid out like some crazy blanket against the stickers. Afterward we left the crushed space we'd made and waded around in the overwarm water, no more than thigh deep, and splashed, and laughed.

I inherited the statue. Twenty years later it stands on a bookshelf, suddenly eloquent, and I almost believe I remember noticing it that first time, wedged there between those ranks and battalions of devils, no more than a foot in height: the deformed figure of a man, grotesque, almost abstract, with huge, amphibious hands and feet, kneeling in supplication before an unseen judge, his head forced to his chest as though crushed from above, like Jesus on the cross except that rather than nailed to the horizontal wood, his hands, monstrous and heartbreaking, reach out ahead, palms out, as though begging forgiveness, or offering them-selves as explanation for some irrevocable wrong.

It has been four years now since my father, noticing the statue perched precariously on the edge of the living-room bookshelf, began talking of the war and a man named Machár, or Macháč, who was said to have huge, outsized hands and whom he thought he might have met once over half a century ago. And I remember the man at the door, the grizzled cheeks, the wisps of uncombed hair, fine as an infant's, and I have no way of knowing if it was him.

The odds are less than small. I never actually saw the old man's hands. There was nothing in his face or manner. The town we had found ourselves in that summer afternoon was nowhere near Jíndrichův Hradec, the town Machár was said to have returned to. And my father, not least, had always been a storyteller, a magician for whom even the most sober handkerchiefs tended to burst into tropical bloom at the slightest provocation. Perhaps there was no Machár. Or perhaps he was a composite—of other men, other stories, of anecdotes overheard, misread, misremembered, from a war already half absorbed by fictions. Perhaps all I had, all I would *ever* have, was a wooden statue with hands as round and deep as a pair of catcher's mitts, chosen from a roomful of demons by a woman I'd once known and cared for.

At the end of every life is a full stop, and death could care less if the piece is a fragment. It is up to us, the living, to supply a shape where none exists, to rescue from the flood even those we never knew.

We all, like beggars, must patch the universe as best we can.

The Woodcarver's Tale

As František Machár was being born into a wooden room thick with the smell of lamp oil and women's sweat, the brittle shelves of ice that covered the ruts on the roads sloping to the river were caving quietly under a hard March rain. Streams and rivulets threaded the meadows, gushed into roadside gutters, dug tunnels beneath old snowbanks, and swept on. The river loosed and groaned. The midwife cleaned up the mess and lowered the lamp. On her way home, she flung the afterbirth to the pigs. It was 1915, the second year of the war. The little boy was the son of the village *lesník*. It would be a year before the father returned from the front.

The child grew quickly, not all that different from the others who survived: tough, resistant, slow to cry and quick to forget. By the time he was five, he was spending his days in the forests with his father. They would rise at dawn in the cold. If it was raining, he would look down at his shoes walking up the dirt road and listen to the rain drumming on his hood like fingers on a wooden table. To keep his direction, he watched his father's legs, the black huntsman's boots with the heavy wool pants tucked in at the top, his father's hand with the tufts of black hair on each finger curled around the heavy, big-bore rifle he had brought home from the war. Where the road ended, the two of them would climb up through the soaking grass, away from the town, the river, to the fogged silence of spruce and pine.

In the forest the rain was diminished, a distant hissing, a spray of mist across his face. The needles and moss would be like sponge beneath his feet. He wouldn't talk, he'd listen, and his father's voice (low, clear, rough as a pine burl) would seem measured to the place, to the creak of trees, the spaces between the wind.

This, rather than any desk or pew, was his source. To him, the things his father's voice explained or touched were scripture; the questions, the answers, a forest catechism; every blood-tipped quill, every broken reed, every flash of color in the gloom, a parable of survival or death. What about this? Machár's father would say, indicating a yellow-stemmed mushroom prodding up to the air, a cap of loam still perched on its velvety head. And the boy would have to recite what he had learned: no skirt, no sheath, gills burned orange and closely layered, swollen like pages left in the rain, a smell like crushed walnuts. *"Dobry,"* he would say. It's good. And his father would dig beneath the loam with his hands, not pleased, and a finger's depth down his thumb would run the rim of a ghostly sheath, thin as membrane. "Eat this, you'll die," he would say to the boy. "Remember that."

Years of stories built around a core of fact. If a *skřivánek* burst from the edge of the meadow, his father would point out the flash of yellow on the underwing, the looping glide. They're nervous, quick to fly, he would say. When you see one, be careful. They tell you something's moving. That flower, bright as arterial blood? It's *vlčí mák*, the wolf poppy. Eat the bulb at the center for pain. And he'd tell him about Petr Vaculík, a logger from Řásná, who, crushed by a freak fall, a wrist-thick branch jammed through his body like a spear, walked out of the forests on a bent-limb crutch, eyes like a saint's, his mouth and chin dark with pollen and a bouquet of crimson poppies clutched in his bone-white hand.

And wood: always the smell, the roughness, the company of wood. His father's saw raining softly, piling small hills of dust: orange, pink, white. The boy would run his fingers over the crosscut, reciting pith, heartwood, sapwood, bark. The pith was the eye, he knew. Heartwood was next, bone-hard and dead. Sapwood was lighter: living cells that would shrink and warp. It would clasp the saw, admit the chisel, endure badly. Oak had clean, well-defined rings. It was strong, flexible, hard to cut, held the nail like a mother her child. Ash had a clear border, a frontier between heart and sap. Beech was reddish white throughout: no heart, or sometimes a false one, soft and unworkable. Good, his father would say, when he had done well. Remember it.

And he would. He would remember it all: the long days, the grasses frozen in the meadows at noon . . . He would remember his own legs trembling down the tilting fields toward home, the evening star like a speck of mica in the blue above the hills, how his dreams would be filled with the sad soughing of trees and the burbling of water and his father's voice asking, "What is it? What are they saying?" and him knowing he could answer, easily, without effort, forever.

They found the severed head of the buck the week before he turned seven. His eyes had caught the dull light of bone before he saw they were teeth, drawn back from the gums, before the head itself had leaped into shape. It rested on the blood-soaked ground in a blue tangle of guts, just off the trail. His father squatted beside it. Poachers, he said. Fanning away the iridescent cloud with the barrel of the rifle, he turned the head carefully over, then turned it back. Looking up, he squinted off into the near distance of the forest. The poachers had left it there for him. To think about.

His father didn't speak but, knowing instinctively that death must be made familiar, deflated, made no more of than what it is, stood, picked a sturdy stick off the forest floor, and jammed it into the cavity of the neck. Hoisting the thing over his shoulder like some ghastly parody of a vagabond's sack, he set off straight across the woods, the boy following, until the random streams of ants crossing and recrossing the trail grew thicker and faster and there, fifty meters ahead, stood a swarming, chest-high mountain of needles set against a spruce. Machár stood there beating the ants off his shoes with a fir branch, watching his father walk steadily toward it, carrying that grisly offering. When he touched the buck's head to the mound, the darkness boiled up like a cloud.

He was eight when the poachers roped his father to a hill just like it in the forests outside Branna, and the world should have jarred on its axis, the sun struggled to rise, but nothing happened. The river ran, the rain fell. No one told him how his father died. No one spoke to him about it. But he knew. And the lesson seemed clear: evil was everywhere, in the sheath on a mushroom, the opaque eyes of a butchered buck, and if you let it in the door, if you died, if things went wrong, it was your fault, your failure. The evil, in some dim way, was yours.

No one told Machár this; he figured it out himself, as he thought his father would have wanted him to. In the spring he and his mother moved away, boarding the train to Brno with a suitcase each, Machár carrying his father's death like a peach pit lodged halfway down his throat. It was in town that his hands, big and floppy as a puppy's since birth, first became a burden to bear. At home there had been the usual fistfights; here his hands seemed a particular curse, and he dragged them on like a badly anchored ship through the tedium of school (*erro, erras, errat*), through the three years at the *průmyslovna*, the technical institute, then the *strojírna* in Žďár. When the war came, he did what he did without thinking about it much. The work of a smuggler came easily to him. And then the war was over.

The peace was nothing. The country gasped for air like a swimmer caught in heavy surf, only to be buried again. Machár married his wife in January 1948. The coup came on February 24. On April 9, young Masaryk, Czechoslovakia's last hope of a return to the days of the First Republic, plunged seven stories from Černinský Palace to the cobbles. Machár's son was born the next winter.

He came first for her, true, but it was for him that Machár left, crossing the open farmlands south of Mikulov to Drasenhofen, then through the Soviet zone to the British sector of Vienna. It was for him that he cut through the fences, at that time still free of electric current, slipped past the wooden towers, slogged miles through the muddy dark toward the Austrian oilfields gusting up like candles in the distance.

Like a fox ferrying pups, he brought her across, then

crossed again, running the gauntlet, returning one last time across the still, February fields, eleven hours each way, for the pinched red face that did not know him, the wisp of black hair, the tiny spastic arms, softer than anything he had ever known or would again in this life. He wrapped him in a gray blanket and started back. The baby was sick. He cried, his small, animal wail sounding through the muffled pines. Terrified, Machár held him close to his chest with his huge hands and crashed on through the crusted snow. It was not until dawn, crossing a vast, white field ridged and furrowed by wind, that he stopped and unwrapped his hands from around the quiet bundle he had held for hours in the warm cave of his coat. It took him a long time to realize the child was dead.

And the world ran out like a marble down a long, dark tunnel, and then there was only silence. And voices, somewhere, trying to talk to him. She left some time later, and he did not try to stop her. It was his fault, he knew, his utter responsibility and guilt, just as it had been his father's, except that his father's mistake had been fast and final and killed only one; his, Machár's, had taken three. He would stop now, on roads, in doorways, his face suddenly collapsing like a child's that has been struck for no reason, and remain there, long after the pain had gone, with that surprised, inward look of a man still listening for the murmur of his own dead heart. For a time he existed in the refugee camps near Innsbruck, then, having nowhere else to go, returned to Czechoslovakia, alone.

When he returned he was arrested, though no punishment had ever meant less to a man. The nine years passed like sleep. He dug potatoes, worked the roads, fought when he had to. On a warm September afternoon, the bus dropped him off at the crossroads, and for the first and also the last time he walked down that long hill and over the bridge with the water clattering below. The house was owned by an uncle he had met once as a boy. Years ago he had heard he was living here. He took Machár in, then died. When no one came to claim the house, Machár stayed on.

And time built its slow rings around his guilt, hardening pain into truth. When a weasel slipped like an eel through the coin-sized knothole in the wall of the chicken house, he read the lesson in the carnage of feathers and blood. He saw it in the torment of a mole batted about by a cat on the front walk, tossed in the air, batted again. In the squeal of piglets eaten by the sows, in the demonic grunting from the pen.

It was not long after Machár arrived that he picked up a hunk of cedar from the splitting log. He turned it slowly, suddenly remembering his father cupping big handfuls of wet sawdust to his face, breathing in the rough perfume. It seemed to him that in the dead solid shape of the heartwood was the suggestion of a face, and he went to the shed for a chisel and hammer, took out his pocketknife, and started hacking him free: small, straight horns, curved nose almost touching the thick upper lip, the rude first progenitor of many generations to come, truer and more lasting than the generations of men.

And that is where he would stay, alone, unbothered, not well but not dangerous, frightening only to children who like being frightened, staggering on under the weight of his days until the morning he tried to rise from his chair at the table and found he could not, then laid his head on the wood by his half-eaten breakfast and died.

And yet this could not have been all. Two, maybe three years earlier, there would have been an October afternoon threatening snow that found him, like every other afternoon, in the workshop, moving carefully through the living cells to the dark striping of the heart. There would be no salvation here. No love. No re-demptive vision of midges suspended above the water and naked children swimming till late in the flatwater by the dam. Only mercy, perhaps: unbidden, emerging as of its own volition with each lifting curl of the unshaped wood, revealing to him, as though for the first time, the faces of those who had worked his father free, beating at the black swarm moving up their arms and legs, then wrapped him in burlap and carried him home; those for whom his father's death had been meant as a warning. Those, so *like* his father, after all, who did not listen. Who did not know how.

It would come back to him in a rush: the woodshed the day after his father's funeral, filled to the roof with cedar, oak, even applewood, aged, split, and stacked. And how every Sunday at dawn, there would be something hung out back, out of reach of the dogs: a pair of ducks tied at the neck, a pheasant, a whole leg of venison. And the old coin sack filled with toys: miniature pine-cone owls with button eyes, twig feet, and wings of leaves; hazelnut mice with hair whiskers and tiny rope tails . . . and sitting there, watching his huge hands doing their work, old Machár could almost hear his father's voice: "Remember them."

And he would remember now too the hand lost in his like an egg in a nest, the one he had dropped that night as he lunged for their throats, the softness under his thumbs coming up against the bone, the clear crackling as of branches when he brought the strength of his shoulders to bear through his forearms, his wrists . . .

And that is where I leave him, years before my life would cross his, in a bare cold room thin with wind, and outside the small pocked window shoved off-plumb into the thick plaster wall, small curled leaves gathering against the clutter of fences and catching in the tangled gardens, not hearing the bang and bang and bang of an unpainted shutter beating the changes, calling the river to frost, not seeing the small aromatic drifts of shavings gathering, spilling off the gullied lap of his blue canvas pants to his shoes (set far apart and sad like the facing cornerstones of some vast, unspared mansion), from them to the cracked and broken floor, knowing only that emerging from the palmed wood was not the same familiar shape, the monotonous affirmation of his guilt, but (see the head bent low to the chest like a resting child, the bending back, the aching, cross-hatched ribs, those huge and haunted hands, palms outward, supplicant) his brave and broken self.

the minnow trap—
a sketch

Sometimes after dinner in the weeks after my grandfather died my father and I would walk through the long
last light to the brook thick with olive duckweed except
by the rock and the crotch of a sunken branch where
the current had gently separated the vegetable skin and
the water showed dark as a beer bottle; the minnow
trap would bounce against my legs, first one end, then
the other, then double time, spinning on the yellow
cord I tried to hold away from my body. There were
always little pieces of muck in the mesh, fern bits delicate as window frost, others like clumps of unwashed

elfin hair. Slick and brown as mud in water, they dried emerald green.

The tree against the end of the pool lay pale against the gloom, hard and pocked as an old bone. It had toppled long before I was born. The roots had disappeared, but the crater in the earth where they'd once levered up was still there, so close to the main water it caught the overflow of every good rain and stayed half full for weeks, stagnant, dimpled with larvae.

"Go ahead," my father would say, "take it over," and I'd jump from the soft bank onto the slick and polished trunk, sneakered and sure, and walk out over that apparent earth, false as the rolling meadows of cloud seen from a plane. My father would wander a few feet up along the water and light a cigarette, watching the current wrap around a car-sized boulder, a branch trembling as though pulled from underneath, the quick swirl of a fish against roots exposed along the far shore . . . I'd hear the sure snap of the match but I'd never see it, watching my feet negotiate the raised nubs where limbs had been, the circular whorls where rot had tried to set in, further and further out until I reached the iron ring he'd screwed into the wood that August, chest-deep in water, cursing when he dropped the bit, then putting in the other he'd left on the trunk as a backup, holding it for a minute between his lips saying, "Don't ever do this, this is a very stupid thing to do, you could cut yourself real bad this way," then trying to keep his footing while leaning into the hand drill, fighting the stubborn wood until it was done.

He'd be standing there on the bank, not watching, the cigarette appearing with each slow draw as he brought it to his mouth, then dropping to his side.

"Okay," I'd say.

"All right, now throw it well out," he'd answer, his voice suddenly turning my way through the dark, spanning the void. "Let the rope loose so it can settle down on the rocks." I'd lob the trap upstream, listening to the crisp sound of the mesh hitting the water, then reading its descent through the cord in my hands, the bumping progress in the gloom as it neared my feet.

"Didn't catch," I'd say.

"Did you remember to put the rock in?"

"Sure."

"Try it again."

We'd walk up the sloping grass together, my father always a step ahead, thinking, his left hand in his pocket, me pushing hard through the sopping, knee-high grass. On the stone porch, unaware, he'd always flick the inch-long butt of the cigarette with his right hand. It would rise and fall in a small clean arc like a stricken star, over the wooden rail and down into the close, wet grass.

In the morning the air would be like damp wool, the

trunks of trees near the water black with wet, growing like props out of the mist along the ground. A
woodpecker—a muffled hammering—a splash somewhere, and I'd be working the knot, listening through
the rope to the trembling of small bodies already
strengthening to a sort of agitated hum as the trap lifted
off the rocks, and then it would touch the surface and
I'd pull it up into the air, the small mesh bottom a layer
of tiny flipping fish like a shimmering mat of silver,
quick with life.

I'd carry them back to the metal bucket on the bank.
Picking through the mass, I'd find fingerling bass an
inch and a half long, perfect miniatures; tiny black
crawfish frantically snapping their mermaid tails; small
yellow and green perch, pretty as Christmas orna-
ments; a dozen leeches lengthening over the screen,
raising their front ends as though to mark their direction; baby bullhead catfish with velvety skin and tiny
whiskers, small as a finger. These last were my favor-
ites. Their dorsal fins were still too small and flexible to
really stick you and you could pick them up with three
fingers like some narrow pastry and look right into their
faces. I liked their flat little mouths, their creamy bel-
lies, their bulgy eyes and pouty expressions. If you held
them like that for a while they'd open their mouths and
croak like tiny frogs, throaty and brave.

I spared them all. I'd show off my haul and after
breakfast my father and I would dump the bucket in

the brook. We could have used them for bait, stuck them on number 8 hooks set just below the fin or through the lips for casting, but I had not yet learned the art of killing my sympathies, and my father, suddenly that summer, had lost the will to teach me.

jumping johnny

Who among us hasn't noticed it, the strange doubling of forms and faces—the echo in the world? The waves in rock, the veins in leaves, the ghostly flowerings of frost. As though god, deep in his labors, had suddenly run out of ideas, or, perhaps, surprised by the loneliness of his creation, had set out, in the eleventh hour, to stitch the world together: the sound of wind to the sound of water, the ruffling of field to the ruffling of fur, the memories of the living to the hopes of the dead. A familiar universe. A sea of small recognitions. A vast brotherhood of thoughts and things. This is what he dreamed.

It was too late. It didn't work. We misread inten-
tion as accident, correspondence as coincidence. Only
rarely, wandering through this world, did we feel that
someone was trying to tell us something.

It had been years since we'd talked, a lifetime, maybe
more, since I'd buried my nose in his shirt as he carried
me, still wrapped in blankets, from my small, wooden
room through the graying woods to the car. It had never
been easy. On the day they brought me home, as he
hovered over me, studying my belly with its little
umbilical tail, my red shriveled legs, still bent to the
womb, my wavering little bud with its downy sack, I
happily peed in his face.

Forty-one years later I was shown into a hospital
room where he lay surrounded by machines, and didn't
recognize him at first. Holding the coat and the small
bag my wife had packed for the trip, I stood just inside
the doorway, looking at the tubes coming out from
under the sheet. From the hallway behind me came a
man's voice: "Why don't you tell him then? Say . . ." followed by laughter and a young woman recounting
something I couldn't make out. I watched the respirator breathe, jerking his chest up, then collapsing it as
under some invisible weight. A young man with a
stethoscope around his neck came into the room and
began checking the monitors. "Are you the son?"

I nodded. I was the son.

"Your dad's looking better. He was convulsing when they brought him in last night." He glanced at his clipboard, though he didn't need to. "Seems he was down almost seven minutes before the paramedics got to him."

My father started to gargle, then choke; an alarm went off from one of the machines by his side. Slipping on a pair of plastic gloves, the man removed my father's mask, swept his mouth with a finger the way one might clean out the bottom of a cup, vacuumed around his tongue with a small suction tube, then replaced the mask. The machine went silent. The breathing resumed.

"Why are his arms and legs tied down?" I asked.

"For his own good," the man said, not unkindly. "Without some restraint, he'd yank everything in sight." He left.

I looked at my father, his face swollen under the respirator mask, his eyes staring at the ceiling like a drowned man looking toward the sun. Seven minutes. I remembered the lake: him slipping under the surface, disappearing like a big white fish into the gloom, gone a minute, a minute and a half, two minutes, showing off, always coming up twice as far out as we expected. We'd cheer and he'd start the long swim back to the dock. A few wisps of hair had fallen over his forehead. I brushed them back, tucking them under his head. Skin

like damp velvet. *"To jsu ja,"* I said, in Czech. "It's me."
His eyes blinked. A look of terrified incomprehension
passed over his face, and was gone. "I'm here now," I
said. "Try to get some sleep." Turning to go, I noticed
the sheet had slipped off his body, exposing his cock
sleeping on his thigh. A tube ran from it to a bag
hooked to the bed. I covered him from the eyes of
strangers and picked up my things.

It was dark when I left the hospital. I could feel the
air—cold for mid-October—move through my shirt. I
breathed it in, held it a long time, then let it out and
started walking: down the shuttered streets to Lafa-
yette and Fourth, past the steel mills looming big and
dark over the river like castles abandoned to plague,
then up along the row houses to the three-story apartment building he'd learned to call his home.

I let myself in, threw my bag and coat on the sofa,
and closed the door. A half-empty glass stood on the
coffee table; a fountain pen lay uncapped across a
blank piece of paper on the desk. I walked to the bathroom, pissed—loudly, aiming for the water—then ran
the faucets, listening to the pipes cry in the walls. In
the kitchen I rummaged around in the cupboards, filled
mostly with paper plates and cups and plastic silver-
ware, and made myself some toast and tea. I sat down
at the white Formica table. Something—a picture, a
memory—so faint it seemed from another life (a man, a
table, no more), moved like a warm wind, momentarily

loosening the hard knot in my chest, and was gone. I sat there a moment. And then I left.

Just past the laundry room, at the end of a hallway lit by a bulb stuck in the plaster ceiling, I found the communal basement: a long cellar, partitioned along both sides into individual cells of chicken wire and two-by-fours. In the third cage on the left I recognized what remained of my legacy: 150 cubic feet of toys and tools and cartons packed around a core of steamer trunks still bearing the stickers marking my parents' departure for the new world. For years he'd been asking me to go through it, to take what I wanted and dump the rest. "You've got to help me with this," he'd say on the phone. "I'm not a goddamned museum. If you want it, take it." I looked at my watch. It was just after two.

I don't know how it is that things come to carry the weight they do, how the sticks still carved and the photographs and the cracked and moldering plastic toys come to seem the very fingerprints of our lives, as though we were, each and every one of us, no more than spirits in a material world, visible only by the things we've gathered and broken and touched. I only know that it's so. I'd made it through the phone call, the deserted terminal, the hospital itself. I'd made it past his face, his skin, his hands. The Jumping Johnny stopped me cold.

———

I found him in the first trunk, pressed between a layer of children's clothes and a crumbling mass of first-grade parchment: leaf tracings and orange pumpkins and a headless turkey with waxy brown and orange feathers still smelling of crayon. The red paint of his pants had faded and one of his legs was splintered and cracked, but the satisfied U of his smile with its little umlaut nostrils was still dark and clear, and I pulled on the partly opened ring attached to the hinge at his back and his arms began waving frantically as though triggered once again by something living deep beneath the ice. And suddenly my chest began to ache and Johnny's smile blurred and swam and I realized, almost to my surprise, that I was crying.

It opened quickly, as memories will, a small window of happiness, pure as ether: my father—in one of those spasms of easy creativity he seemed to resist throughout his life—jigsawing a rough little man out of a piece of stained plywood he'd found in the barn; the two of us (I was no more than seven), fat with coats and hats upon hats, lying side by side on the deck chairs we'd dragged onto the ice, hamming it up, pretending to tan; my father suddenly leaping up as Johnny began to wave, running madly across the ice—or wanting to run, dreaming of running—but instead slipping, flailing, falling, or bouncing, rather, first left, then backward like some rubber mannequin, cursing, laughing—I can hear him still—finally diving belly-down on the ice, sliding swaddled and friction-free into home, closer, then right past the little man now seemingly intent on nothing more than trying to flag him down.

Everyone has theirs, I suppose. More than all the others, more than the ones we planned and prepared, I remembered that day: my father's sudden, inexplicable happiness, the two of us on our knees, dropping the hook with the stiffening minnow down the coffee can–sized hole we'd chopped into the ice with a chisel, then peering down into the gloom. (And suddenly, sitting there in that cellar of things, I felt it again, a warm rush of happiness like a shot of hard drink on a cold night, then gone.) I looked at the Jumping Johnny on my lap. An icy fog had kept moving out of the forests all that morning, erasing the shoreline, then gradually penciling it in again, and one by one we laid the perch that Johnny caught for us on the ice next to him (their barred yellow sides the only bit of color in all that frozen world), and my father, clowning on the ice, made me laugh so hard I snorted hot chocolate from my nose. He was scared of nothing that day. He was my father and my friend and he had biceps like big navel oranges when he rolled up his shirt and he was scared of nothing.

And now he was scared. And I couldn't help him. He'd caught me, covered me, drawn me out of danger a thousand times, but when his turn came, when his heart seized and cramped and he fell, following his own falling drink past the counter and the table legs to the carpeted bottom where his own glasses with the thick dark frames already waited among the chards like strange black coral, I wasn't there to pull him up. And now, trapped on the other side of a canyon full of dials and tubes, I couldn't reach him. All I could do was watch him drown, or keep myself busy going through an old cellar at the end of the world, sifting memory from trash.

There is some salvation in this: even in the worst of times, there is the next moment, the next thing. The clock ticks, the stomach grumbles. This is what happened next. I put aside the Jumping Johnny and scooped up a double handful of clothes and papers and old magazines: my own thirty-year-old shirts and pants and jackets, smaller than the ones my son was wearing now; my parents' letters, packed and densely scripted, still in their *Luftpost* envelopes; the dog-eared issue of *Life* magazine commemorating JFK's assassination. And there, underneath a toolbox, I found Graumont and Mansel's *Encyclopedia of Knots for Boys*. I'd gotten it for Christmas the year I turned eight. I lifted it out and opened at random to the bowline, then the blood knot, then the hangman's noose—and suddenly I could feel the tumblers falling, and again the image I'd been pursuing like a grail since I'd left the hospital—a man sitting at a table, at dusk—lifted my heart and was gone. But not entirely.

Here is what I remembered: autumn dusk and the hissing of damp wood in the fireplace and the smell of dill and onions coming from the kitchen and my father, already on his third drink, sitting next to me at the dining-room table overlooking the lake, trying to help me through the bowline and the clinch knot—up comes the rabbit, then down into his burrow—the water just outside the window so close that when the wind moved the leaves, the room, like a houseboat, seemed to drift anchorless along the shore. And suddenly my father, halfway through the hangman's noose, complaining of something stuck in his throat but already reaching for his coat and walking out the door, my mother instinctively calling out from the kitchen, "*Co je?*"—What's wrong? "Dinner's almost ready"—then coming to the table, glancing at the open book, the looped rope in my hands and saying quietly, "C'mon, help me set the table."

I didn't ask. I put the Graumont and Mansel on the end table by the soft gray couch on which my father slept at night, and then a few days later moved it to the bookshelf in my room. And that was that. An only child, you see, I was accustomed to the ghosts that could send my mother to the bedroom, weeping, or my father out to the chopping block for an afternoon or more, and I knew enough to stay out of their way. In our home,

the past was always present, a landscape as familiar—
more familiar, in some ways—than the one through
which I ran and played. Born in New York, the immigrants' son, I knew the low sky and the slate-red roofs
of Brno and Prague long before I saw them, heard the
silence of fields, cultivated since Rome, long before I
stumbled in their furrows, smelled the smell of court-
yards at dusk—the wet-sand smell of lumber and
coal—long before I leaned out of actual windows, a
foreigner smoking a cigarette, recalling a place I'd
never seen.

And so, when I realized that my book of knots had
somehow stirred what needed to be left alone—some
memory of home, or war—I put the book away. It
would be fully fifteen years before I found the puzzle
piece, in the shape of a letter my mother had written to
a friend, that completed the picture. My father was just
sixteen when, in the so-called Fuehrerhaus in Munich, Chamberlain and Daladier tossed Czechoslovakia to the Germans like a piece of meat to a pursuing
dog; barely twenty when German troops poured into
Bohemia and Moravia; not yet twenty-one when, newly
married, a cub reporter for *Lidové Noviny*, he was
forced to cover the public executions at a small, shady
square off the town's center once known for its farmers'
markets, now given to a different harvest.

He never quite got over it, said my mother, years
later, who, hardly twenty at the time, got to meet him at

the door that first evening, got to hold him, breathing in the slight, lingering smell of his vomit, got to feel him shake and heave in her arms like a frightened child. Sometimes, she said, the process took two and three and four minutes, the victim lurching and thrashing as in some mad, antic dance, the small crowd, mostly women, some with young children in their arms or on their shoulders, laughing and pointing . . .

As a child, I remembered, I'd touch the appendectomy scar that pulled in the skin on the right side of his stomach. It looked like a man sucking in his cheeks and felt strange and smooth against my fingertips. I was fascinated with it—with its drama and ugliness—but most of all, with the fact that he'd gotten it when he was only twelve years old. This was of no small importance. I knew twelve-year-olds. My father's body, incredibly, had once been like mine. I would be like him. But looking back now, I could see there was more. That I unconsciously touched that scar—as my own son now touched the fat white strip on my arm—the way a pilgrim touches a holy relic. Seeking absolution for the sin of innocence. Or acknowledging, by way of the surrogate flesh, the accumulated scars unavailable to view.

And there were a few. Not an exceptional lot, perhaps—there were some who bore worse—but vivid enough, "creative" enough, as it were, to justify a drink or two or three as the years came on, to explain the inability to loop and snug a length of clothesline into a child's knot. Cowardice? Maybe. But I'd never watched the stain of fear spread on a young man's pants, nor watched him dance and die at the end of a common rope. I'd never had to imagine, as my father had, his own father's head passing through the noose.

It happened like this: twenty-four years after the evening I closed the Graumont and Mansel, ten before his heart gave out, my father, newly divorced and drunk on the back lawn of our suburban house, told me that *his* father, a spy for newly formed Czech legions operating with the Allies in Italy, France, and Russia, had been hanged in 1917. The Austro-Hungarian front had been moving quickly, he said. Retreating north, they had left the cherry trees along both sides of the road thickly strung with executed legionnaires; for a full three kilometers, they dangled from the fruiting branches like the pupal sacks of some ghastly insect.

Watching my father's hand shake as he brought the glass to his mouth, listening to the muffled clicking of the ice cubes, I approached the thing as delicately as possible.

"But Dad," I said, "Grandpa died when I was eight, remember?"

"Do I remember?"

"But you said . . ."

"I know what I said. I said they hung him. I didn't say he died."

I was silent for a few seconds.

"I didn't say he died," my father said again. He picked up his glass, shivering in the hot sun. "They were in a hurry, the bastards. They had a lot to do."

"So . . ."

"So he managed to kick around till somebody cut him down, that's all."

The story came out slowly during the course of that drunken afternoon. How my grandfather, a cobbler with the face and charm of a dissolute duke, had found himself, at the age of twenty-two, suddenly marching south through warm rain to the Italian front, chosen for service in the espionage unit, sent over the lines, and, just as quickly (the whole thing must have seemed strangely accelerated, as in a dream) standing on a ditched, hardpack road with his arms tied behind his back, watching a man he'd never met construct a nine-loop noose on the end of a pale brown rope.

He knew exactly what was going to happen (by the time they came to him, after all, he'd watched forty or fifty others hoisted on the same horse which was then neither slapped nor spooked nor jerked away as in the movies but simply led off toward the next tree until its burden had slipped from its back) and yet, in spite of this, he went quietly, disbelieving, even as the noose was being slipped, almost gently, over his face, even as he felt the horse walking out from under him. The instant before his legs slid off the horse's back, before the sky and the leaves and the dark fringe of trees on the horizon began their mad, tilting dance, he noticed a bunch of cherries—tight-skinned and fat—on a low, dripping branch a meter from his face.

He jerked and thrashed like all the others—it must have made quite a sight, my father said, that three-kilometer alley of trees—except that after the others had stopped, he was still going. Seems they'd either left too much rope, or the branch had bent just enough, or the sides of the ditch in that particular place were just a bit narrower than elsewhere. In any case, when the Allied front came through later that afternoon, two men on horseback, one on either side of the lane, went from rope to rope with their bayonets, dropping the dead like huge fruit into the ditch. Grandpa was one of them.

Except he wasn't. Waking during the night, like some mud-soaked Jesus from his own personal Golgotha, he crawled out of the ditch, cut the rope binding his wrists on a scythe he found leaning against a haystack, and started walking. Three weeks later he was home. The only thing he had to show for it, said my father, who was born six years later, was a miniature tremble in his handwriting, as though his feet, leaving the back of that Austrian work horse, had tripped some invisible switch, starting—just a bit too early—a strange, nervous current, like death's own heartbeat. That was it, my father said. That and a photograph, the torn-off cover page of a magazine, in fact, that hung in the parlor throughout my father's childhood: inside its gray handmade frame, below the white lettering of the magazine's name, *Domov a Svet,* it showed a wet country lane stretching to the horizon, cherry trees, and two converging lines of the dead. A journalist traveling with the front, apparently, had taken the picture before the cavalry cut the men into the ditch. Browsing a stationery store less than a month after his return, my grandfather recognized himself as the fourth man on the right.

Pouring himself another drink, my father looked over our burned-out lawn to the anemic row of poplars bordering the yard, pausing so long I thought for a moment he'd lost the thread of his story.

"He had this magnifying glass," he said at last. "Big wooden handle, big glass . . . every now and then he'd lift the picture from the wall, sit me on his lap, and show me, just a millimeter or two from his face, a tiny cluster of spots no larger than the grain of the picture itself. You could see them there against the clouds—

the very same cherries he'd noticed the instant before they hung him. The last thing he should have seen on earth."

I said something more, but my father, lost in the near distance, was no longer speaking to me but to someone else: his own personal amanuensis. Or *his* father. Or god himself. I wanted to reach over, to wipe the fine sheen of sweat from his forehead. I couldn't move.

My grandfather, he said, would sit at the kitchen table, sometimes till dusk, picking cherries out of a white bowl with his work-hardened fingers, carefully spitting the pits into his hand. Gloating. Looking in from the doorway, his eight-year-old son could see the picture lying flat on the white tablecloth next to him; at that angle, he said, it looked like a small, dark window, or a fishing hole in winter ice.

A familiar universe. A sea of small recognitions. A vast brotherhood of thoughts and things. I set the Graumont by the Jumping Johnny, left the cellar as it was. Outside the street was gray with light, a photograph in the developing tray: gutteredge and rail and wall. I started walking.

Two days later, when my father awoke from the morphine and demanded his pants and his cigarettes, when the doctors spoke of the heart's fibrillations sometimes continuing to carry oxygen to the brain as though operating on memory alone, I knew that a different kind of memory had kept him alive: the memory of a man at a table at dusk. As though the son, looking up to the light, had seen a familiar face. As though the father, seeing how things were, had reached down to his drowning son and borne him to the light one last time.

the exile

It was nearly ten when I finished bailing the boat, and the moon, rising over the eastern shore, sat perfectly full on the trunk of a broken birch. The sky was opening quickly. I placed the disjointed rod against the wood and undid the rope, listening to the trees along the shore dribbling into the water. In the woods behind my back a pale, slanting room, its walls and ceiling open, its floor carpeted with leaves, showed where the moon had cut into the darkness.

Her name was Maruška but everyone called her Marie and I remembered her, though it had been thirty years at least since I'd watched her (a fourteen-year-old hidden in the shadows by the shore), slowly row her boat across the open field of sky on a night no different from this one. She was a tall, almost pretty woman with no one to tell her so, a woman who worked hard at happiness without, it seemed, ever quite knowing what it was. I liked her. Though she was older than my parents, she seemed, at times, strangely young to me: a sad, precocious child trapped inside a grown-up's body. She'd speak to me in Czech when we met on the path and kid me a bit without making me feel foolish, but even I couldn't help noticing that her laughter, as she sat on the float with the others, her knees drawn up, always seemed to stop just a bit sooner than anyone else's, or that in the middle of things she'd suddenly look down as though seeing something under the water's surface, then quickly glance up to see if anyone had noticed.

Women liked her, advised her, spoke for and over her. Men—even those who, like diviners, sensed some depth beneath the surface—lost their bearings before her silences, her conspicuous lack of artifice. Her guilelessness showed no seam; her sadness, no source. She was all of a piece, unapologetic and whole, and this frightened them, and their wives, recognizing the danger in this, quickly fired up the moat of condescension and kindness. As she grew older, of course, as her breasts and thighs grew slightly heavier and younger ingenues warranted more of their husbands' attention, they let the fire burn itself out; a few, in fact, discovered that they quite enjoyed her company now, that what had once been false—a self-protecting ritual—had now become genuine and true.

I worked my way along the eastern shore, casting into the bars and stripes of light coming through the trees. A doe and her fawn, backlighted by the meadow, stood poised and still, stenciled against the pale grass. "Marie Kessler?" Virginia Hass had said to me that afternoon, when I asked. "You mean the one married to that writer? She died last fall, I believe. Or maybe the year before that, I'm not sure. I'm surprised you even remember them. You were just a boy then. They moved to Pittsburgh, I think, soon after the trouble that summer."

I'd hardly known her and yet, I'll confess, it was strange to hear she was gone. Somehow, I realized now, I'd always imagined her here, all the years I'd been gone myself, as though her story had made her a part of this landscape, irreplaceable as any wooded rise or croaking meadow.

I raised the oars. The cicadas and the katydids had been starting in the trees since the rain let up, and now a great rhythmic sawing filled the night. Ten thousand tiny throats were calling in feverish unison from right over my head, ten thousand more from the opposite

shore: urgent, intoxicating, relentless as surf. Thirty
years ago, crouching in the shadows of the shoreline
trees, I watched her row away from the yellow lamp
under which her husband sat reading, saw her stop, tilt
her face to the moon, then slowly run her hands over
her cheeks, her throat, her breasts. The insects raged
and screamed. When she lifted the oars again, I'd
followed.

Josef Kessler was just forty-seven when he noticed
her—her hair, her simple dress, opened at the throat,
the slight tilt of her head—in the second row of the
amphitheater at Masaryk University in Brno. At the
reception following his lecture (which he had agreed to
as a special favor for a childhood friend), he introduced
himself. Though they spoke of music, specifically, his
passion for American jazz, she, like everyone else
in that room, knew the facts. By the age of twenty-
seven, Kessler had been an adviser to the president; by
thirty-five, one of the intellectual pillars of the First
Republic; now, after six years in exile with his family,
one of the most powerful and respected figures in
Czechoslovakia—a man of undeniable courage and
grace. She was not yet twenty-two, a first-year student
newly arrived at the university but already gaining a
grudging reputation among the faculty of the School of

Philosophy (with whom she stubbornly refused to sleep) as a writer of surprising passion and depth.

They spoke. He was charming. She listened, mostly, watching his face, aware that something was happening, powerless to stop it. He apologized, explaining he had to catch the ten o'clock train back to Prague. She shook his hand. Six months later, in a move that made the front pages of the Prague papers, they were married. Josef Kessler left his family, resigned his post, retired to private life—fully prepared to spend a year or two writing, advising, patiently playing his hand from behind the curtain until the day when he might once again regain the public sphere. His young wife, newly ensconced in a spacious, sun-filled apartment off Old Town Square, swept up by something very much like love, left the university and Brno and learned to enjoy the not insignificant pleasures of music and conversation and wine in the company of people whose names invariably graced the next morning's papers.

Whether Marie Kessler, in time, would have found happiness in Prague, I have no way of knowing. It's important to say (though it complicates our story), that she felt neither seduced nor stifled, that she cared for her husband, that she respected him (or, at least, respected the extent to which others respected him), that she enjoyed seeing his pleasure. Clearly, he was fond of her, and, with her own family less than a half day away, she returned often with her husband's blessing, walking the forests, swimming the ponds she'd known as a child. Entirely solid, contented lives have been built on less.

It all happened with tremendous speed. In the dream she would remember the rest of her life it was night and she was leaning out the window of an unlit train, waiting for it to leave the station. The wooden platform was empty, a stage set under a single cone of light. She felt thirsty. Suddenly a man she had never seen before walked quickly out of the station, his long black coat lifting behind him, and she said something as he passed and he looked up and smiled and she started humming a tune—an obscure folksong her mother used to sing—and he was humming it with her, and suddenly he was more familiar to her than anyone had ever been in her life: she felt she'd known his broken nose, his dark hair, falling over his forehead, the shape of his hands and fingers, for untold ages, and without a word she leaned out the window and kissed him even as she became aware of a sound she'd been listening to, without being aware of it, for some time—a rapid, urgent knocking. Looking up the tracks, she saw the conductor, annoyed, leaning out of another window three cars down, rapping on the side of the train with his knuckles. "Close the window," he yelled. "I can't," she lied, feeling the train shift beneath her. "It won't close." Again the train moved, strangely, as though floating on water, and turning back to her lover she kissed him again, desperately this time, feeling something changing, shifting, feeling him slipping away into something very like death, and again the conductor knocked, louder this time, the sound thundering now across the empty platform, and suddenly she was awake in a diminished if familiar world, the apartment filled with sound, her husband, pulling on his pants, already at the door.

A rough-looking young man in a long brown coat stood in the doorway, letting in the frigid air from the hall. He spoke to them both briefly, handed over a fat, unmarked envelope, excused himself, and left. It was December 19. They'd been married one year and two days. Twenty-four hours later they were following a hired smuggler (a sullen, brooding man who appeared at the rural inn they had been directed to and stood unmoving in the doorway, hands jammed in his pockets, while they collected their bags) through the bitter dark of the southern forests and across the Austrian border. She remembered little: the squeak of snow; the precut hole in the border fence; the vague form of her husband, just ahead, insisting at first on carrying their single suitcase, finally giving in to the smuggler who, for all his initial awkwardness, moved through the woods with the ease and strength of a big cat, took his pay at the edge of a field within sight of an Austrian train station, and disappeared.

Two weeks later they were in Paris; three months after that, New York. The truth of it is that she hadn't wanted to go. When word had come that the coup was imminent, that her husband would soon be arrested, that to save himself years of imprisonment— or worse—he needed to leave, yet again, the country he loved, she had balked. They had talked all that night, the envelope with its directions and false documents on the coffee table between them like a silent third party. He was convincing, urgent. He wouldn't go without her. If she decided to stay, he said, he'd stay with her, and take his chances. He meant it.

As always, she watched him as he talked. He seemed to her intensely alive that evening, energized by the crisis, like a boxer beaten once, eager for a rematch. Exile, he argued, was as fascinating as it was frightening, as much opportunity as threat. America would show them something new and, after all, the situation wouldn't last forever—two, three years at the most. Soon enough they'd be back. They had to decide, quickly, now. She resisted, argued, finally cried. (Perhaps she'd begun to guess even then that she didn't love him; had begun to realize that to him she was a detail—an important, perhaps even essential detail, but a detail nonetheless—in the larger drama of his life and times.) The small space where the curtains failed to meet began to pale. What if things didn't change? What if this was forever? The clattering of a trolley hushed by cold came from the street below. "Very well," he said, slipping the envelope like a thin volume onto the bookshelf, already adjusting to the new situation, "We'll stay, my dear."

She left. She left without seeing her parents or her brother or her things, the village or the woods or the ponds she'd known. Her leaving was a sudden death, and in her memory, everything froze: the smells of alfalfa and dung; the dust on the roads that she'd run as a child, her ribs tight against her chest; the leaning stable where she'd lost her virginity to a *cigan*, a gypsy, a beautiful young man with smooth brown skin and soot-black hair who entered her gently and spilled himself across the straw on which they lay; the pasture where she'd found her father, bleeding from the mouth, the day he was kicked by the plow horse. All these and more—the scent of herbs, the language of gestures, the particular fingerprint of each season's shadow and color, in sum, her home, her youth—all these she carried with her across that snowed-in border like invisible, precious luggage no smuggler could ever help her with.

And the door closed behind them. The new regime, neither more nor less brutal than expected, settled in. In six years, one letter arrived, smuggled over the border by a mutual friend. Her husband, a chameleon by choice, not weakness, capable of blending through sheer will into any background he chose, adjusted first to the size and speed and hustle of New York, and then (as the realization that they might never return began to dawn on them both) to the permanence of their situation. Happily substituting Duke Ellington for Dvořák, Horn and Hardarts for the cafés of Malá Strana, he forged ahead, creating a life for himself along the way. Sitting on our porch at the lake, a bottle of scotch on the table next to him, he would draw diagrams on a paper napkin with a fountain pen, trying to convince my father of the uniquely European virtues of American baseball: "The field isn't grass, Mostovsky, it's memory itself," he'd say, the anglicized names with their hard consonants protruding like stones from the stream of fluid Czech. "DiMaggio forever sliding into home against Ernie Lombardi in '39. Bob Feller pitching a no-hitter on Opening Day at Comisky Park. The individual game means nothing. History, tradition, is all."

Of course, by the time he found himself discussing baseball and drinking scotch on our porch in the new world, twenty years had passed, and much had changed. At some point along the way, I suspect, Josef Kessler, like a man speaking to his wife at a crowded fair—pointing, commenting on this and that—had turned around and found himself alone. Neither unintelligent nor particularly insensitive, it must have come

as a shock to him to realize that he'd left his wife standing ten or twelve or fifteen years back in the snow of the
Austrian border; that as he and the smuggler had
moved on, she'd turned to look back, and frozen with
grief; that the woman he'd lived with, talked to, made
love to for a decade and more was a ghost of sorts, pal-
ing with the years.

There was no point in talking about it. To return, he
knew, would be madness: a guaranteed ten years,
maybe more, in a communist prison for both of them.
Apologies were also useless, nor, in fact, had anyone
asked for any; there was no way he could have known
then that what appeared most likely to be a two- or
three-year spasm would drag on for decades. Or a lifetime. No, what had happened had happened, and the
best they could do was acknowledge the situation, then
move ahead and make the best of it.

Still, recognizing the heart's resistance to reason,
Josef Kessler did what he could. Hearing of a lake not
far from New York, an old-world pond with twenty-
three wooden cabins populated by a motley group of
Irish- and Italian-Americans, Czechs and Poles and
German Jews, he decided to rent a cottage. The place,
he hoped, might, by small degrees, gain her love; might
become, in time, a reasonable replacement for the
world she'd lost. With the years, even, it might suddenly blossom—it was possible—so tenderly that his
wife would find herself won over: the past, finally and

forever, would fall away. The present moment would rule over her heart.

Though she woke late that particular morning, the air moving through the screen was cool, the insects quite still. She lay quietly on her back for a while, covered with only a single sheet. A lightning bolt of sunlight lay across her legs. A single jay screeched from the shade somewhere, the sound chill and clear. As a girl, she would like awake in bed, looking out across the mustard fields. She remembered how her body had felt then. It seemed odd to be nearly fifty. The years had shot by like chips in a flue, irresistibly rushing toward their destination. There had been nothing to slow them, nothing that needed her love. A forest suddenly appeared against the wooden wall, brightened—the individual leaves rising sharp and dark as though from under water—then faded quickly.

Outside, on the stone porch, she could hear the heavy, sumptuous snap of the *New York Times*, the small collisions of cup and saucer. Her husband, she knew, had been up since five, writing. At eight o'clock he had capped the pen, made himself a cup of coffee, slipped the paper from where a neighbor had wedged it between knob and frame, and retired to the porch. He never glanced at the paper early, never quit before eight, never sat in the Adirondack chair with the solid arms, preferring the rickety one she'd painted green two years before.

"Good morning," she said, speaking up to the ceiling.

Outside, the chair creaked, the paper rustled. She knew, without seeing him, that he'd closed the paper, folded it twice, then turned partway around the high back of the chair to speak toward the house. "Good morning," he said. "You're missing a beautiful day. Coffee?"

"Mmm," she said.

"You should see the paper. This Nixon thing is beginning to gather momentum. By the way, we've been invited for drinks at two."

"Already?"

"Goldstein rowed by this morning, getting his exercise."

Marie Kessler was moving her head, trying to find the source of the bolt lying across her legs without breaking the fragile envelope of warmth surrounding her body. At that moment something splashed far out on the lake; she could distinctly hear the two-part concussion of the body hitting the water, the chest and arms followed a split-second afterward by the feet slapping down. Curious, she sat up in bed. A swimmer had dived off the float—which was still rocking gently—and was now cutting a bright V across the tight surface of the lake. She watched him play, now sliding through the water with slow, powerful strokes, now rolling on his back, squirting thin streams through his teeth, graceful as a porpoise. Returning to the float, he lifted himself effortlessly out of the water. She watched him shake his hair like a dog, then throw himself on the wood already warming in the sun.

From the porch she could hear her husband's dry chuckle, three puffs of air escaping the nose, no more. "Youth will be served," he said.

She would have been the first to recognize the cliché: a childless, middle-aged woman, not so much unattractive or uninterested as simply, quite reasonably, beyond all that (ready now for large sun hats and sensible clothes and the steady compensation of small, expected pleasures), making an utter fool of herself over a man—a boy, really—just exactly young enough to be her son: a boy with eyes like a cat's drowsing in the sun and a mouth just slightly cruel; a boy, above all, superbly, effortlessly fit, his every movement an affront to age.

But so it was, and there was no one on the float later that August afternoon, regardless of age, who didn't sense the sheer force of it, who didn't feel at least some awe in the face of an attraction so unlikely, so abrupt, so utterly undeniable. It wasn't subtle, it wasn't slow. Kessler, a trim, attractive man at seventy-two with his white mane of hair and white tennis shorts, brought the rowboat alongside and slipped the rope over the post of the ladder, then held the boat still for his wife. The others were already there, laughing, talking, some in beach chairs, some lying on towels, all nursing drinks in wicker holders. He lay on a deep-blue towel, quietly dripping water, twenty years younger than the youngest there, unaware or unconcerned that he was in the way.

Someone made a gesture and she came over, stepping carefully over the arms and legs and drinks, and he moved aside for her, not so much moving himself as just pulling in the edge of his towel a bit to make room for hers. Virginia, in her own way, introduced them, leaning over Goldstein (already arguing good-naturedly with Josef Kessler) and calling across the float: "Marie, the attractive young man whose towel you're sharing is Anthony Musker. He's the brother of that nice young man who moved into cabin twelve with his family a few weeks back. Anthony's watching over things for them." Marie Kessler, drawing her knees to her breasts, nodded a quick hello. Young Anthony, still lying on his back, breathing hard from his recent swim, turned his head and regarded her for a moment. Behind his sunglasses, she could barely see his eyes, moving over her face. "Pleased to meet you," he said, not smiling. She looked away, accepted the drink being handed to her. A child—muscular, lean—probably the terror of undergraduate virgins at some local community college.

They said later that Marie Kessler drank too much during the course of that afternoon, that by four o'clock she'd had one too many glasses of the Chablis my father kept chilled in an ice bucket under a wet towel in the rowboat, that this was why she behaved, well, the way she did.

They were wrong, of course, or only partly right; like religious naïfs who substitute a bauble for the glory of god, they mistook shadow for substance, a small intoxication for a vastly greater one. The fact is that, forced into proximity by the crowd around them, they started to talk. He asked her about herself (a young man's questions—personal, often quite tactless—about her life, her dreams, whether she slept on her back or her side . . .), and she answered him, at first, in the mildly amused, slightly condescending tone women of a certain age will employ to keep attentive young men they suspect of being merely polite in their place.

But even as she spoke, laughing off some question or comment, now and again glancing toward the others to see if someone else would enter the conversation and relieve the young man of his duties, she found herself, quite to her surprise, enjoying his company. He laughed easily, listened well, seemed genuinely curious about everything she had to say. They seemed, more often than she would have thought likely, or possible, to agree on things—important things. Her idealism, her sense of outrage, always slightly embarrassing to their circle of friends, found a receptive and enthusiastic audience here, and, in spite of herself, she found herself moved by this. He seemed, instinctively, naturally, protective of her.

An hour passed. Then two. The shadows of trees began to extend from the western shore. The sun, well past its meridian, seemed mellower now, sweeter than before. At some point, Josef Kessler, feeling slightly guilty for having abandoned his wife, glanced up from his conversation. She was sitting shoulder to shoulder next to a young man who seemed to be listening intently to what she was saying. The two of them were holding their knees, their heads tilted toward each other, nodding, smiling now and again (like children at a picnic, Kessler thought), and, pleased that his wife, who often seemed so out of place at these get-togethers, had found someone to talk to, Josef Kessler turned back to his friends.

When someone dived into the lake, rocking the company on the float, Marie Kessler was surprised to find that three hours had passed. It was nearly five. Someone had rowed back to the shore, and now a plate of hors d'oeuvres was making its way around. Her husband, in a heated debate with old Rheinhold Černý (where had *he* come from, she wondered), suddenly seemed far away.

To her left, one of the Bartlett sisters was saying something—to her, she now realized.

"I'm sorry?"

". . . a little sandwich, Marie?" Joan Bartlett was saying, passing over a plate of small, open-faced breads.

"Yes, yes, thank you. They look delicious," said Marie Kessler, passing the plate to her right. Anthony's hands, she noticed as he took the platter, were brown from the sun. He looked away quickly.

Marie Kessler and Anthony Musker sat next to each other, silent for the first time, as though suddenly aware of what had been happening to them, as though suddenly conscious of the intimacy they'd found— of the space, like a warm blanket, that had slowly wrapped itself around them over the course of that afternoon, separating them off from the crowd. For a moment, and a moment only, they felt naked in each other's company, and perhaps, at that instant, one of them might still have broken the spell. But neither moved, and the moment passed, and when their eyes met a few seconds later, when he moved to make room for someone passing on his right and his thigh momentarily touched her knee, she felt a soft trembling current run through her as distinctly as though he'd touched some cord, some secret wire, unprotected and bare.

"C'mon, let's go for a swim," he said, suddenly, as though she were nineteen, as though she were in the habit of just diving off the float rather than climbing cautiously down the ladder, the skirt of her bathing suit slowly spreading like a spent blossom around her, and seeing him leap and crash into the water, she followed, and before she knew what was happening the lake was coming up around her and he was there and splashing playfully, teasing her, and the water, warming in the evening air, was dark and smooth, and when he suddenly disappeared under the surface and tugged her under by the ankles, she screamed his name in surprise and splashed him, laughing, when he came up for air.

Even in the retelling, it smarts like a slap. How the two of them returned to the float, sometime later, only to find it oddly quiet and emptying quickly, the atmosphere thick with decorum and the strained casualness of people determined to show their good breeding by not taking advantage of someone else's social embarrassment. No less than five people went out of their way to say good night to her personally and to tell her that they'd see her in the morning, and her husband himself, already sitting in the rowboat, spoke to her with the terrible civility of a parent addressing an ill-behaved child in a public square: "Come along, my dear, it's getting late. I think we've all had quite enough fun for one afternoon."

She was furious, of course, indignant, and her husband, neither a fool nor a monster nor even incapable of love (just incapable, perhaps, of loving her), found himself pressing the only advantage he had—the truth—all the while knowing, pathetically, that it would not be enough. That his reproachful silence would avail him nothing, his attempts to shame her, only feed a fire that had been slowly devouring itself, drawing in the walls, suffocating, like a blaze in an airless room, for decades.

And now, suddenly, the blast of cold, clean air: like fall, like rain, like life itself. And why should she care who it was exactly that flung open the window, who kicked down the door? And what did it matter? Through the open rooms of her heart the fire raged and stormed, and how could it not, in its gratitude, consume them all? I imagine she recalled, with a mixture of embarrassment and wonder, the quick frown that passed over Anthony Musker's face when she stepped, chastened, into her husband's boat, his defiant "Good night, then," as her husband pushed away from the float. I imagine she remembered bits and pieces from that afternoon: his smile, the warmth of his skin, the arc of his body entering the water; that as she ate her dinner, she wondered (like a schoolgirl, she thought, like an absolute schoolgirl) what he was doing, who he was with; that later that evening, naked in the dark under the outside shower, smelling the crushed mint growing between the boards beneath her feet, she recalled the broad curve of his back as he turned to reach for a book, the smooth muscles of his thighs and calves, the small, tight package pressed between his legs, its shape just outlined by the wetness of his suit . . . and barely breathing, in an agony of remembered need, lifted her breasts with both hands to a lover even then sitting three hundred yards across the water, looking toward the shore.

Everyone could see him, all that next afternoon, reading, swimming, waiting on the float. Just before six, he rowed back to shore. An hour later he was back, sitting cross-legged by the boat, sipping a cup of coffee, fully aware, and utterly unconcerned, that everyone on that lake knew he was there. The next afternoon, he was back; and the one after that. When she walked outside on the third night she could see the bulk of his boat, still tied to the ladder, blocking out a boat-shaped space in the reflected stars. The float itself seemed appropriately named, adrift in a medium no thicker than air. It was just past midnight.

On the fourth day clouds rose and burst. The lake, roughened under the rain, turned the color of stone; the float, reflecting sky, was empty. Far from making things easier, his absence made them infinitely worse. Agitated, nearly on the verge of tears, Marie Kessler cut herself with a bread knife across the soft skin at the base of her thumb. It took a long time to stanch the flow of blood that kept flowering on the paper towels she held to the wound and dropped like crushed flowers on the kitchen counter, and her husband, concerned, offered to drive her to the hospital for stitches. She didn't hear him. Shortly after ten that night, Marie

Kessler abruptly got up from the couch where she had been reading and walked into the humid dark.

Crossing the stone veranda, she took off her shoes and socks and slipped them under the Adirondack chair, then stepped down to the path leading to the shore. The rain had stopped, though everywhere around her the soaking woods still dripped and splashed. With the leaf mulch sticking to her feet, she walked out onto the narrow dock. The sky was clearing quickly. Before her, pressed between sky and sky, lay the shores she'd known for almost ten years, perfectly doubled like some exquisite, troubling Rorschach, its ink still wet.

She knew what she was doing, of course. Would have insisted on knowing. Would have taken in everything, every detail, with an almost hallucinatory attention: the way the reflected moon, troubled like a tuning fork by every mayfly's touch, would quaver and break its strange white yolk, then draw it back; the way the strokes of her oars, like tracks pressed in some quicker soil, would silver for a moment, then quickly go black. And more: would have noted, and ignored the fact, that the single fisherman suspended where the shore's dark palisades dropped abruptly into starry space (or anyone else walking out on their small wooden dock for that matter) would be able to see her row—brazenly, unashamedly—toward the lamp burning in the window of her lover's cottage.

I don't know why I followed her that night; perhaps,

even at my age, I sensed something in her manner—an intoxication, a rapture—that fascinated me, and moving quietly through the open patches of light between the trees, I cut north across an open meadow, then ducked down again toward the shore. Her boat, as though swallowed up by the night, was nowhere to be seen. I came down low to the cattails, thinking I might see it more clearly against the sky. Nothing. I turned quietly along the trees, expecting to find the boat anchored somewhere under the overhanging branches, and nearly stumbled over them. First frightened, then confused, ultimately mesmerized by their passion, I crept back into the dark, then turned to watch.

Stepping barefoot into the warm, soaking grass, the insects screaming in the shoreline trees, Marie Kessler had barely started up the slope of the lawn when suddenly he was there, holding her, his hands following the straps of her dress from her shoulders to her wrists, then quickly over her hips. Pulling her down to the soaking grass, he lay against the wetness and she moved over him, a lover suddenly young again, noticing as from some distant place the shock of his skin against hers, the warmth of his breath in her hair, his mouth sucking at the cut on her hand.

It's possible, I suppose, that if they had only stayed low on that open lawn, everything might still have passed. But that, I realize now, was neither her way nor her desire: never again would she hesitate on a border.

And so, feeling her lover start to lose himself beneath her, Marie Kessler placed her hands on the small of her back and sat up straight into the moonlight. And who but those who have never risked the visible world for dreams half done and gone, could ever hate or blame her?

night—a sketch

I heard something die in the swamp last night. It rose quickly out of the silence, a hoarse, agonized screaming, low and guttural at first, then building to a series of piercing shrieks, and I left the sagging couch and walked to the window, staring past the legions of small, white moths crawling up the screen, as though I might somehow see whatever it was being torn down there in darkness thick as paint.

But the sound didn't stop, one moment fading like a guttering candle, then rising again, until finally, unable to think of anything else to do, I found myself looking into the little wooden room where our daughter slept, clutching a soiled kangaroo, our boy next to her (the small hollow of his throat etched as clearly as though he were watching the stars in his dreams), all the while certain the sound would wake them, frighten them, and I'd be unable to stop it or explain it away or shape it with any fairy tale fit for a child.

And then, for no apparent reason, I began to grow afraid. Not of the prosaic truth—a snapper dismembering a duck or goose in the slick black muck, or a mink, feral and quick, killing a family of muskrats in the briars by the shore. Not that. Of that sound. My throat tightened; the muscles in my back and neck, in that strange mirroring of passion and fear, stiffened and tensed, and I stood there, staring past the door we'd opened against the heat as though something might come through it, listening to the gurgling and the thrashing and, underlying it all, an orgasmic, boarlike grunt like a ground tone about to explode into some as yet unwritten, unimagined crescendo, and then it was over and a single cicada somewhere high in the trees rose like a fever.

Later that night I awoke from strange, disarticulated dreams and knew, as though it were some great truth the world must instantly be told, that the ancient oracle had been wrong, that the old gods were alive and well, and the Dionysian dark, older than our stories, bigger

than death, existed just outside the screen of our cus-
tomary days.

The next morning my son, barely seven, woke me
with a damselfly he'd saved from the lake. It sat, sod-
den and bent, its abdomen protruding through one gossamer wing, at the end of his little finger ("You know,
this damselfly is a very brave person," he explained),
and all I'd dreamed and thought the night before suddenly seemed distant and foolish and wrong. And I
guessed at that moment the grain of our fate, the particular shape of our exile: to sense, at dusk or in
dreams, the route to our own redemption, the harsh
truth of the earth's equilibrium, its eternal economies
of birth and blood, but to know that path as forever
closed to us, rightly obscured by our hearts and lies.

"You take care of her," I said, still waking. "Damselflies turn into fairies at night." Half an hour later, I
found him crouching on a boulder in the morning light,
watching her dry her mangled wings.

the lotus eaters

We called it the moonhouse, though it had no moon, having been built thirty years ago by a busy man with no feel for poetry. But moon or not, the Finnsmiths' moonhouse had presence. Character enough. Nodding slightly forward, eager to please, it leaned just enough to give its visitors the sensation of sitting in a very narrow room on a very narrow ship. The space itself could only be described as intimate. Lean forward too precipitately—to pull down a pair of trousers, say— and your head would hit the door, which, delicately secured by the merest point of a badly placed hook and eye, and encouraged by gravity, would promptly swing open.

And then of course there were the residents: spiders of various sizes and temperaments; small clouds of gnats that hovered over one's head like the comic-book smudges meant to signify deep thought; paper wasps tending their carefully masticated little buds under the eaves . . . To sit there—vulnerable, half exposed, a clammy bathing suit around one's ankles—was to feel the nudge of mortality, to suspect, if only for the barest moment, the utter frailty of human conceits.

But this is not a story about the moonhouse per se, but about the moonhouse as an agency of the gods. The vehicle through which they, on a particular September afternoon in 1966, revealed their divine will.

In those days we lived in Canarsie from October to May, migrating inland just as the water was warming in the shallows and the hills leafed into summer. Billy Finnsmith would be waiting there when we drove up in our dented blue Rambler, when we pushed open the cabin door—closed for six months, swollen in place— when the scent of grass and honeysuckle swept into the corners smelling of mildewed wood like some high-speed re-creation of summer's victory. And he would be there a full season later, framed in the rear window, watching us bump and scrape down the dirt, leaving boarded windows, a double-locked door, and two chains swinging slightly in a new wind as though still holding the memory of the love seat now propped against the couch in the cottage dark.

The months in between our coming and going I would spend at the Finnsmiths' cottage, a more or less permanent visitor in a house that seemed to me straight out of some disordered fairy tale: cheerful, messy, utterly unconstrained by the conventions of the world outside its covers. If my mother worried occasionally that I was overstaying my welcome, she was the only one. I attracted no more attention than the box turtles hunkered down under the sagging sofa or the white rats, Sacco and Vanzetti, who lorded over the kitchen counter, expertly turning crusts in their thin, human hands. If there was food enough, and I was hungry, I ate. If not, not.

Define it as you will, theirs, I'm convinced, was a charmed existence. When Billy and Lilly (who were ten and seven at the time), set the dining-room table on fire while their parents were off collecting mushrooms, they threw water on the table (and the curtains) and the fire went out. They didn't suffer terrible burns over 85 percent of their bodies. The baby didn't die of smoke inhalation in his crib. Nothing happened. Mr. Finnsmith planed the burned edges off the table, then collected the whorled shavings and gave them to the kittens, who later stitched tiny black pug marks all over the stones of the outside porch. When little Bean, just over a year old, crawled off the end of the dock and fell headfirst into the mud (it was an unusually dry summer that year, and the shore had receded ten yards out), Billy and I happened to walk by while his legs were still wiggling like some weird, antic buoy, and pulled him out. He didn't suffocate. The trauma didn't warp his character, leading him, years later, to a life of brutal crime. Mr. Finnsmith gently hosed him down. Mrs. Finnsmith cleaned the mud out of his ears and nose with a Q-tip. An hour later, there he was, butt-naked on the stone porch, holding on to a low branch with one hand, happily gumming a drumstick.

Irresponsible? Reckless? Perhaps they were. Mrs. Finnsmith, I recall, spent most of her time reading novels aloud to the various children sprawled around her in the oversized hammock or conducting (there's no other word for it) the absurd riot of flowers on the south wall of the cabin. On cool summer mornings, when the spirit moved her, she'd rig a parasol to the oarlock, sit little Bean (naked as always) on a stack of *New York Times* business sections, and go visiting. When the baby wet itself, soaking through the New York Stock Exchange, she'd calmly peel off the soiled layers and put them in a bag. At night she'd sit cross-legged by the fire, her dark hair shining in the light of the flames, and scare us silent with wonderful, tangled stories of ancient times and grand adventures and ghosts both cruel and kind.

Her husband, for his part, spent his days fishing, painting (there was always paint—ocher and eggshell and rust—crusted in the hair along his temples and the stubble of his jaw), or cobbling something together in his work shed. Every now and then he'd climb with us to the top of the elm and hang there, barefoot and shirtless, swaying in the high wind.

This, I see now, was the land of small pleasures, of present time. Ironic, irreverent, generous, the Finnsmiths depended on no doctrine or dogma, believed in no dietary plan, aspired to no utopian perfection. Humor, companionship, the world of the senses neither strenuously denied nor excessively indulged— these were enough. The result was a strange and wonderful equilibrium, a balance bordering on magic. No one who knew them, I'm sure, could have guessed how difficult their accomplishment really was, how fine the fulcrum, how delicate the balance of their happiness.

John Finnsmith, for all the years I knew him, was a man continually distracted by eternity; sooner or later he'd balance nearly every species of work against the weight of mortality, and find it wanting. Far from making him gloomy or morbid, this point of view (admittedly somber from the outside) made him an unusually cheerful man. It ordered his priorities. "He spent *how* long doing that?" he'd ask, incredulous, when told of some acquaintance newly emerged, dewy-winged, from the chrysalis of schooling or apprenticeship. "Five years? Jesus!"

If he was lazy, it wasn't in the vulgar, plebeian sense of the term. He painted, when time allowed, with rigor and passion. He'd taught himself Latin. An amateur ornithologist, he wrote to Roger Tory Peterson suggesting some changes in the description of the head markings on Henslow's sparrow. I'd seen him work a twelve-hour day painting three-hundred-pound rowboats he'd dragged from the water on a system of home-made winches and pulleys. No, his was a rare, distinctive condition; a sort of spiritual hemophilia. Unlike the mass of men and women who apparently suffer the cuts and indignities of their chosen occupations with relative equanimity, he seemed incapable of enduring work he found uninteresting or unimportant. Every now and then he'd try—pathetically—to talk himself into it, to justify and reason and rationalize, but it was no good. The wound wouldn't clot. He'd endure for a time—then quit. The Finnsmith family would breathe a sigh of relief, and life would tilt back to plumb.

Which is not to imply that it was easy, that in an age given over to climbing metaphors—to ladders and rungs and pinnacles—Billy's obstinately earthbound father did not come in for his fair share of grief. The problem, in sum, was this: John Finnsmith didn't get up at 5:45 every morning in order to catch the 7:12 out of Brewster; he had nothing to say about stock options, company dividends, or the goings-on at shareholders' meetings; no one had ever seen him in a tie; in his personal pantheon, Henri Matisse and Theodore Gordon (the destitute dean of American dry-fly fishing) sat supreme; Adam Smith held their palette (or patched their waders). All this would have been at least somewhat socially digestible, perhaps, had he only been sorry or sheepish or envious, or, better yet, had the good grace to suffer from some redeeming physical or psychological handicap—alcoholism, for example, or some debilitating nervous disorder. But John Finnsmith, unaccountably, was neither sick nor sorry.

"The problem with John Finnsmith," explained Mrs. Alice Ebner-Hauptmann, for whom other people's shortcomings seemed something of an avocation, "is that he's got no vision, no goals. You'd think he'd want to better himself. But bettering yourself"—and here she'd begin to punctuate her words by poking a forefinger into the rickety Adirondack chair in which she sat, her eyes behind her dusty cat-frame glasses bulging like a frog's squeezed by some nasty child—"bettering yourself takes work."

"Hard work," agreed Eugenia Bartlett, her comrade in criticism.

"Hard work," echoed Ebner-Hauptmann. "Stick-to-it-iveness. Once you start something, you have to stick with it until the end. Nobody said you have to like it."

"Exactly," said Bartlett.

"What men like John Finnsmith need is what my Richard had in spades—*Sitzfleisch*."

And having settled that John Finnsmith was entirely destitute in this department, and that the best thing for him would be a major if not tragic crisis, something to acquaint his nose with the great grindstone of honest labor, they settled back with their Bloody Marys and shifted their crosshairs slightly to the other members of the Finnsmith clan.

Overall, however, the winds of criticism blew lightly over Billy's father. It helped, of course, that Mrs. Finnsmith, an intelligent and unusually attractive woman given to wearing loose cotton dresses into her husband's workshop at odd hours, had an entirely different take on the importance of *Sitzfleisch*, and thought about stick-to-it-iveness not at all. Mrs. Finnsmith, it seems, had her own priorities, which Mr. Finnsmith, always rushing home from some part-time job or other, seemed to amply share.

But every bloom will have its bugs, and theirs was no exception. The spring Billy turned eight, his father, hard up on forty, sauntered, Job-like, onto a particularly rough patch. His generally successful overtures to the curious world of art galleries and shows began

returning with the monotony of messenger pigeons—
rejected. Bills long buried and forgotten returned from
the dead, suddenly unpaid. Money, always elastic, now
turned stubbornly resistant. Things seemed to search
him out from afar just so they could expire at his door.
And suddenly, like a high-wire artist looking down,
John Finnsmith wavered. He'd been wrong. He had
nothing. For twelve years he'd played the proverbial
grasshopper, singing his lungs out, and now the ants
were going to eat him for dinner. He had to do something, anything, and quickly.

Those long accustomed to basking in the sun of
health and good fortune often take the slightest
cloudlet personally—a sign of divine displeasure if not
outright castigation. So it was with Billy's father. He
paced, he raged, he agonized. He thrashed around like
a tiger in a tar pit. In a more demonstrative age, he
might have rent his mantle, and defiled his horn in
the dust.

And then his back gave out. This was the last straw,
no better than boils. Instantly reduced to shuffling
old age, Billy's father betook himself outside to sit—
figuratively speaking—among the ashes. Billy's mother,
meanwhile, left alone to take care of little Bean, followed the drama of her husband's crisis of faith with
something less than divine patience. Their days grew
dark; the house, ripe with the perfume of diapers.
Annoying little midges appeared out of nowhere and

hovered about the bedroom. Mr. Finnsmith, grim, sat staring into the middle distance, mechanically rubbing his forehead along his receding hairline.

Into this, with supernatural timing, came Simon Brand.

Silk-shirted and eau-de-cologned, he appeared on the path bearing gifts from Saks, from F. A. O. Schwarz, from Milt's Bagels. Billy and I had been digging a tiger trap near the compost heap (with Mr. Finnsmith in a beach chair nearby, directing our labors), when we looked up and there he was. Gold sparked at the edge of his sleeve, catching an errant sunbeam. In the frames of his sunglasses, far off, as in some distant land, I could see our world: toy trees, a lilliputian cabin, a tiny Billy picking his tiny nose.

"Ask your daddy if he'll let you play with a new toy," he said, producing a remote-controlled tank roughly the size of a medium-sized dog.

Billy looked at his father. Mr. Finnsmith nodded.

"Now ask your daddy if he's got anything in particular against fresh bagels and nova."

Billy's mother appeared in the cabin doorway. She'd managed to throw on a dress and put on a bit of makeup. "Hello, Simon," she said.

Simon Brand had been placed on the earth, apparently, for the sole reason of putting Mr. Finnsmith's teeth on edge. It was a basic effect, elemental: he drew his ire the way the moon draws the tide. It wasn't just the fact that twenty years ago he'd apparently been one of Mrs. Finnsmith's college beaus, or that the romance had supposedly been—however briefly, however unsatisfactorily, however long ago, and however insignificantly—consummated. Not that alone. At twenty, shortly after being asked to leave the university (following an elaborate point-shaving scheme that suggested, at least, a certain knack for statistics), Simon Brand had inherited a strategically positioned gas station in White Plains. By twenty-five he was well on his way to being a millionaire. By thirty he'd made a name for himself as a publisher of religious and motivational books and records. By thirty-six he'd owned (and sold) a fast-food franchise named after himself, been named Mamaroneck Entrepreneur of the Year, and made a killing in real estate. Worse, he wouldn't go away. Coiffed and capped, aggressively fit, he would periodically reappear, emerging from the climate-controlled womb of his Cadillac eager to share his good fortune.

He was impossible to offend. Simon, it often seemed, operated on a different frequency. Wit was useless against him; irony, still worse. Billy's father, who years ago had reckoned overlong the looks Simon gave his wife, found himself helpless. Throw him out on his ear? Simon brought gifts. Simon told jokes. Simon, clearly, lived to please. Did he offend? It was inadvertent. To resent him would be ridiculous; to feel threatened, a pathetic self-indictment. No, there was nothing left for Mr. Finnsmith to do but chest up to the fact that this particular suitor, having attached himself with lampreylike devotion, wasn't going anywhere anytime soon. In normal times, this was a realization John Finnsmith could live with. But these were not normal times.

Simon Brand was pointing to a piece of butcher paper freighted with smoked salmon. "Have some more, kid," he was saying to Billy. "Here." Reaching over, he piled the soft meat on Billy's bagel. "Anyway, DrayCom's had quite a year. Did you catch the piece in the *Journal* last week? Never mind, doesn't matter. The way I see it, and McCormick agrees, we're a step away from being able to write our own ticket."

"So what's all this got to do with me, Simon?" said John Finnsmith.

"Well, that depends." Simon Brand looked at Billy's mother, then paused strategically. "How does vice president in charge of concept development at Brand Industries grab you? Say, thirty, thirty-five to start?" Quickly raising his hand like a traffic cop to forestall any questions, he continued: "You don't *have* to know anything about the business, John. In fact, your ignorance will be an asset, a plus. I want someone—and please don't take this the wrong way—who can see things from what we in the business call a need perspective; in other words, someone who might himself benefit from a few words of inspiration. In short, John, someone like you."

Sally Finnsmith looked at her husband, as sure of his answer as she'd ever been of anything. John Finnsmith was nudging a plastic lid along the table with his cup, first one way, then back. When he looked up, his eyes met his wife's. He looked down again.

"Don't do it for yourself, John," Simon went on, sensing an advantage. "Don't do it for me. Do it for your kids. Or Sally." He paused. "Look, I don't want to get personal here, but how long do you two think you can keep camping out like this?" Simon Brand waved his arm, taking in the garter snakes in the goldfish bowl, the canvases against the wall. I mean, this is fine when you're eighteen or twenty, but . . ."

"Can I see your watch, Simon?" Billy said. We'd been staring at it. It was big. Gold.

"What, this?" He hesitated.

"You don't need to see Simon's watch," Billy's father said.

"Please, Simon?"

"Did you hear what I . . ."

Simon laughed. "Sure, kid, go ahead."

It slipped over his wrist like something animate and folded, heavy and warm, in Billy's palm. The dial gleamed. The hour and the minute hand, slim minarets of tiny glittering stones, were about to meet.

". . . a time you want to pad the edges a little bit," Simon Brand was saying to Billy's father. "Buy the kids some new toys. Or Sally a new dress."

"We're fine, Simon," said Billy's mother. "Really."

Billy's father, grim, his big forearms on the table, was sucking on the right corner of his lower lip.

"Sure you are," said Simon. "I just meant—"

"When did you have to know by?" said Billy's father. Mrs. Finnsmith turned, staring.

Simon was wiping his big white hands in a wad of paper napkins. "Today, amigo." He stood up—tall, trim, in control. "Look, why don't you two talk it over a few minutes." Not looking at me, he waved the watch back with his fingers. "You still using that outhouse out back?" he said, looking around.

He walked out. Billy's mother waited, poised, like a sprinter in the blocks. "Have you lost your mind?" she whispered, before the screen, sagging on its tired spring, had moved halfway through its arc.

"Could be," said her husband. "Who needs it?"

"You're actually going to go through with this? Inspirational publishing?"

"What choice do I have?" With the thumb of his left hand, Mr. Finnsmith started picking at a callus underneath his right index finger, then looked at his wife. "Maybe he's right, you know. Maybe it's time we woke up. I figure in three, maybe four years, we can . . ."

"Four years?"

"Everybody has to pay a price for the things they want."

"I thought that was what we were doing."

"Look, at some point you stop wasting your time painting pictures nobody wants and you get a regular job."

"Jesus, listen to yourself."

"I'm tired of listening to myself." Billy's father shook his head, then looked at his wife. "I just don't think I can say no this time, Sally. It's too good."

We sat quietly over the wreckage of bagels and bags, of rudely scraped containers and napkins stiff with cream cheese. It was over. Done. The leg was in the snare; the trapper, club in hand, relieving himself in the bushes before finishing his work. Everything would be different now. Billy's father would leave on the 7:12, return in the dark after dinner. He'd wear a tie. The margins of our days, like autumn light, would narrow, then fade.

But it was not to be. Ever unsuspecting, Simon Brand strode confidently through the dappled light to the moonhouse. He opened the door. The wasps growled from under the eaves; the spider bobbed and twitched. He closed the door behind him, knocked it open with his forehead, closed it again. He placed his lean derriere on the plastic seat. And dropped his watch.

I imagine he snatched at it as it descended all winking through the dim, moted light—and missed. Its slim, minaret hands flashed once, and the watch disappeared into the dark space between his legs. Just like that. The moonhouse gulped and splashed. The spider played a little pizzicato on the web overhead.

We were still sitting around that table like stunned peasants in some latter-day Bruegel when Simon Brand appeared at the door. He had the confused, inward-looking stare of a somnambulist searching for his bed.

"It's not insured," he said.

Billy's father looked up.

"My watch," said Simon Brand quietly. "I have to get my watch."

For a moment, no one said anything. Mr. Finnsmith was the first to understand. "You don't want to do that, Simon," he said, as kindly as I'd ever heard him speak to Simon Brand before.

Simon Brand smiled a terrible smile. "What do you suggest, John?"

"If you've dropped it where I think you've dropped it, I suggest you let it go."

"You do, John? You suggest I let it go?" Gliding forward, Simon Brand leaned on the table, sunglasses perched perilously on the rising wave of his hair. "Let me make something perfectly clear. *My* watch is at the bottom of *your* outhouse. I want it back. I don't care how you do it. I don't care who you call. You understand? This isn't some fucking game we're playing here. That watch is worth four times the value of everything you own."

Billy's mother looked at her husband.

Mr. Finnsmith leaned back in his chair. "Was," he said.

"What?"

"Was," said Billy's father again. "*Was* worth four times the value of everything I own."

Simon Brand stared, the veins in his neck bulging against his collar.

Mr. Finnsmith took a sip of cold coffee. "Billy, if you dropped your favorite marble down the outhouse, would you go after it?"

"Yuck," said Billy.

"Lilly?"

"Gross," said Lilly.

John Finnsmith looked up at Simon Brand. "Let it sleep, Simon. There's not a watch in this world worth a trip down the hopper."

But life, they say, is an ordering of priorities, and one way or the other, we pay for the order we choose. Billy's father would never be a rich man; Simon Brand could never let it sleep. The sum of his life thus far demanded he do what he did next, and if—as he and Billy's father walked to the shed, where he was to gather the tools for his quest—there was a certain air of disbelief about his features, it was because he recognized himself, in some dim way, as his own judge and jury. He himself would stand on the scaffold; his own hand would spring the trap.

And that's how it came to pass that Simon Brand,

ashen-faced, found himself standing by the moon-house with a crowbar, a butterfly net, and twenty feet of half-inch manila. I remember it all: how he pried the lid off the well and propped it against the outside wall, the seat like a lidless eye now staring toward the lake. How he probed the depths with the fragile butterfly net like some lepidopterist in hell, hopelessly sweeping that dark, inverted sky. How, finally, abandoning all hope, he . . . But no. Enough.

Billy's father, may it long be remembered, offered to hold the rope. But some things, apparently, a man must do alone. Simon Brand wanted only privacy, and the Finnsmiths magnanimously respected his wishes. But Billy and I, possessed of youth's natural tolerance for the humiliation of others, observed all through a knot-hole in the outhouse wall.

Simon Brand never found his watch. He passed from our lives. He vanished like a vision of the night.

Billy's father's luck turned. Little Bean started sleeping. The sun of self-sufficiency—if not fortune, exactly—shone again. But Billy and I, like dreamers who wake to remember not so much the details as the import of their dreams, would remember Simon Brand for some time to come. We basked, we sang, we avoided all manner of work that might lead to lucre—and whenever the sleep-deprived sons of brave Odysseus appeared on our horizon, we chained ourselves to the rocks of our world to resist their siren song.

equinox

Balance. Symmetry. The bubble at plumb. The tide, poised between ebb and flow. All around us the world conspires against it: the level moves; the tide churns; happiness dies. Only rarely, in courts beyond our knowing (where pleas are heard and bargains struck), do the scales hover and slow, and momentarily come to rest.

I. Ed Sipka

Ed Sipka broke off a piece of rye bread and carefully wiped the chili out of his bowl. He liked the broad, white streaks, like brush strokes, that appeared as he cleaned the juice away. Though he never realized it, he always cleaned his bowl the same way, wiping toward himself in neat semicircles, first the right side, then the left, dropping down through the sedimentary strata of meat and beans and gravy. Tilting back in his chair, he patted his brown beard carefully, then tossed the napkin on the table.

"Goddamn it, Miss Mary, you do make some serious chili," he said to his wife, who had collected their bowls and was carrying them into the kitchen.

"You tryin' to flatter me, Mr. Ed?" she called back.

"Could be."

"And what might you be hopin' to get, sir, flatterin' my chili that way?"

Ed Sipka turned around in his chair. "Depends," he said. "Whatcha got?"

Mary Sipka returned to the room with two cups of coffee. "I think we got about half an hour to kill before the baby's sleepin'. Think you can hold out that long?"

Ed Sipka looked out past his own reflection into the September dark. A warm, gusty wind was picking up, tossing the trees by the road. Upstairs he could hear the big maple scratching like a claw against the shingles. "Is the door to the hallway closed?"

His wife nodded. "It won't wake him up."

Outside, a large gust shocked the trees and quickly

subsided. Ed Sipka frowned. "I should have trimmed it back when I had the chance."

Half an hour later Ricky opened the door, cried, "Honey, I'm home," and abruptly disappeared. The light in the kitchen and the lamp on the end table went out. Ricky's broad-voweled Havana English, sucked into a point of blue light, lingered momentarily, then winked into darkness. For a moment, Ed and Mary sat next to each other on the worn, brown couch.

"Well, shit," said Ed Sipka, with feeling. "I guess I'll get the—"

At that moment two things happened. In the darkness, the phone rang. Then the electricity returned. The lights switched on, the room leaped into view. Mary Sipka turned down the volume on the television. Picking up the receiver, Ed Sipka glanced at the set. Ricky, out cold, was being carried to the sofa by Lucy and Ethel and Fred. Without the soundtrack, the scene seemed strangely desperate, Lucy's face a tragic mask.

"Yeah," he said into the phone. "Sure. Okay. Twenty minutes." He hung up. "Shit," he said again, quietly this time.

Mary Sipka watched her husband pull a pair of boots and a heavy yellow-and-gray rubberized coat out of the hallway closet.

"What kind of trouble?" she asked, quietly.

"Branch in the lines. Billy says it's puttin' on quite a show." A strong gust pounded against the window, followed by a sound like the scattering of small pebbles against the panes. It was starting to rain. Upstairs, like a persistent animal locked out of its home, the claw scratched and scraped against the bedroom wall.

"So why can't the regular crew take care of it?" said Mary Sipka.

Her husband finished lacing his boots and stood up. "They're probably short this week. Ronnie's at his brother's wedding up in Albany, Miller's sick . . ." He shrugged. "Just one of those things."

Slipping into his coat, he noticed the look on her face and took her in his arms, wrapping the coat around them both. She was a small woman, and the top of her head barely reached his collarbone. He breathed in the good, clean smell of her hair, the smell he knew from their thousand nights together, from the times he'd wake in the dark, the two of them tangled together, and just lie there, quietly breathing her in. "Wait up for me," he said. "Maybe we can still have some time for ourselves before the baby wakes up."

"I will," she said.

Before he reached the door, after he'd gone upstairs and (holding back his coat to keep it from brushing forward) leaned over the crib and kissed the humid little cheek next to the pacifier, she said, "Be careful. Don't get bit."

"I will," he said, as always. "I won't."

It was raining hard. In the small backyard, a circular mud bath marked the place where the little plastic pool they'd bought that summer had killed the grass. He sat for a moment in the dark cab of his pickup, listening to the hammering on the roof, then turned on the ignition and bumped down the driveway. He didn't think to look back.

Slick with leaves brought down before their season, the Old Croton Road looked like a beach after a storm tide, littered with debris. Ed Sipka drove carefully, veering into the opposite lane to go around the bigger branches, peering through the windshield that instantly turned opaque as bathroom glass after every hapless swipe of the blades. Around a curve a mile from town, in a densely wooded section across the road from a large Victorian with a wraparound porch, he found the trouble. In the glare of the spotlights, with the rain coming down in long, pale streaks and the wind gusting wildly, the scene appeared strangely cinematic, like a hand with a dagger suddenly illuminated by a bolt of lightning. The branch, he now saw, was actually the limb of an oak fully half again as long as a school bus. At its fractured base, where it had splintered into pale, jagged points, it was easily three feet in diameter. Thirty feet farther up and out, its branches were thrashing in the lines. A massive shower of sparks, as from a welder's flame, rose and fell with every gust, raining down to the ground far below. Off to the side he could see McCourt, huddled small under the hood of his raincoat. Ed Sipka took a last sip of coffee from the cup he'd wedged between the hand brake and the seat. Then he stepped into the rain.

It was not that he minded being the one to go up, though he'd always preferred going up the poles with the belt and the hooks to hacking around in a hydraulic-powered bucket. Nor did he particularly mind working with the big saw; he'd done it before, more than once, and, when all was said and done, better him at six-four than Ronnie or one of the others. Nor, finally, did the weather trouble him too much. Aside from having to watch his footing on the wet metal floor and keeping his eye on branches whipped around by the wind, there wasn't much to worry about.

No, what troubled him, he had to admit, was the sheer mass of that trunk, the angle of the break, even the sloping shoulder of the road along which the hydraulic rig was parked. That and the unavoidable fact that these were big lines: that 25,000 volts, humming like some huge, easily agitated hive, surged through them every moment of the day and night, and that this hive, having been disturbed at its labors an hour earlier, was angry now. He realized this kind of thinking didn't make sense: he'd worked on the lines before, dozens of times, and in conditions no better than this; what was more, this time, with only a little cutting back to do, he wouldn't even have to get all that close to them. A fairly straightforward, up-and-down job. Still, as the bucket jolted and he began to rise, squinting up through the rain, he reminded himself, like an experienced drunk walking himself home, to take it slow. "Easy now, asshole," he said, ducking the dripping branches like a prizefighter. One thing at a time." And then, for no particular reason, feeling foolish: "Don't get bit." Leaning the saw against the rail, he kicked it up, pruned off some of the smaller branches in his way, and went to work.

Four minutes later, according to weather reports issued the next day, the wind gusted to a high of fifty-three miles an hour, and the limb began to go. Hearing the crackling, like gunshots, beneath him, feeling the bucket under his feet start to tilt, slowly, inexorably, as though he were standing in the crow's nest of a foundering ship, Ed Sipka only had time to heave the useless saw away from him before a sprung branch caught him hard across the face and the bucket pitched violently down, then forward into the humming dark. Instinctively reaching out, hoping to grab a branch before the rig went off the embankment, Ed Sipka's hands closed not on wood but wire, and long before his big, charred body hit the ground, the furious hive had shot him through and thundered on, instantly stopping his heart.

II. *Nina Mazzola*

"Touch that I'll kill you."

"You better not."

"Hey!" yelled Paul Mazzola from the kitchen. "Knock it off, you two. Anyway, I saw Dan Colby over at the store the other day, and he said—"

"Well, I will."

"I'll bite you. I'll hit you with a—"

"Hey!" yelled Paul Mazzola again. "I said knock it off. And go wash your hands, it's almost time for dinner. Is he eating this stuff?" he said to his wife, scooping a cupful of suspiciously red-colored dogfood into a heavy, mustard-yellow bowl under the sink.

"Of course not. Regular dressing okay?"

"I said leave it alone!"

"So what did Colby say about—"

"Daaaad!"

"Goddamn it." Paul Mazzola threw down the red-checkered dishtowel and stepped into the living room. "Tommy?" he called. "Get your butt in here. What the hell's gotten into them lately?" he said to his wife over his shoulder.

"It's that new school," said Alice Mazzola. "I don't like it."

After a pause, a little boy, perhaps seven years old, stepped out of the back room. Behind him, his younger sister, her straw-blond hair cut in rough bangs, peered out through a crack in the door, watching to see what would develop. "You too," said Paul Mazzola. Barefoot, overalled, she stepped out behind her brother.

Paul Mazzola looked at his children. Tommy scratched his left arm and was still. Nina, also known as Peanut, picked her nose.

"I'm sorry," said Tommy.

"I don't want to hear you talking like that to your sister, young man," said Paul Mazzola, sounding suspiciously like his own father.

"Or anyone else," called Alice, from the kitchen.

"Or anyone else," said Paul Mazzola. "And as for you, I want you to stop pushing your brother's buttons. You understand?"

"Yes."

"Sure?"

"Yes."

"Then wash your hands and come to dinner."

Only at rare times did he sense it in its entirety, and even then only briefly, as though a love so great, so overwhelming, could only reveal itself in glimpses, could only be seen, like the sun, through some earthly, filtering medium or screen. Often as not, that medium, Paul Mazzola had noticed, consisted of the hands and ears and ribs and knees and knuckles of his children. Nothing more. Like a bumpkin in a museum, suddenly smitten by art, he could feel quite overwhelmed at times by the skin under their chins or the warm, stale breath of their sleeping, and it helped enormously to live with someone who not only shared his infatuation but who seemed equally incapable of expressing it, who could only stare (at what they'd made, after all) and, struck dumb, shake her head. In short, Paul and Alice Mazzola loved their children the way most of the world's parents love theirs.

Paul Mazzola, halfway through his chicken and rice, had barely tasted a thing. "So anyway," he said, punctuating with his fork, "Colby said to talk to this woman—"

"What's her name again?"

"Fiedler. Stop it. Colby told me, pretty much straight out, that he thought she'd be able to get us the loan. Pull in your chair. Seems he knows this couple in town, Sipka or Sitka or something, who—"

A forkful of rice, en route to Tommy's mouth, showered into his lap. Alice Mazzola leaned over the table and pushed her son's plate against his chest. "How many times do I have to tell you to pull your plate closer?"

"I don't know," said Tommy.

"Well, I don't know either."

"Know what?" said Nina, who hadn't touched her food.

"What?"

"When I grow up I'm gonna have two girls and zero boys."

"How do you know?" asked her mother.

"I'm going to talk to my belly."

Paul Mazzola looked at his daughter, at the tangle of straw-blond hair, the stubborn jut of her little chin. She was sitting on her ankles. "Well don't worry about talking to your belly anytime soon," he said. "Eat your food, Peanut." Then, to Tommy: "Is that a fishing lure?"

"Yeah."

"Do fishing lures belong on the dinner table?"

"No."

"Why are you messing with fishing lures when you're supposed to be eating your dinner?"

"I don't know."

"Stop."

Paul Mazzola turned to his wife. "So anyway—"

"Know what?" said Nina.

"What do you say when you interrupt?" said her mother.

"Excuse me."

Alice Mazzola sighed. "What?"

"Know what Chop-Chop says?" Chop-Chop, an imaginary baby snapping turtle, had only recently made an appearance in the family circle.

"No. What?"

"Chop-Chop says I'm old enough to go swimming."

"Not without your water wings," said Paul.

"But Chop-Chop—"

"And never without Mommy or Daddy," said Alice.

"But Chop-Chop *says*." In her eyes, her voice, the downturn of her mouth, the first sign of tears began to appear.

Paul Mazzola put down his knife and fork. "Look, I don't care what Chop-Chop says. We've been through this before." The eyes began to swim. The mouth set.

"She's going to cry," announced Tommy.

"No, I'm not," yelled his sister.

"Until you learn how to swim, young lady, no going out on the dock without me or Daddy," said Alice. "And that's final. You understand?" Silence.

"Nina?" said Paul Mazzola.

Almost imperceptibly, his daughter's tousled little head nodded ascent. After a moment, Paul Mazzola turned his attention back to his dinner. Outside the window, the lake lay still as water in a pot. On the opposite shore, beneath a sky still bruised from last night's storm, the trees had begun to blur together. "Think we'll ever be able to complete a sentence around here?" he asked his wife.

"Can I go to my room?" asked Nina.

Alice looked at her daughter. If stubbornness were a more generally recognized talent, she thought, her daughter would have the makings of a prodigy. "I doubt it," she said to her husband. "Okay," she said to the thirty-eight-pound little girl with the inverted knuckles and the stickers on her overalls—her breath, her life, the unacknowledged axis of her soul. "Go ahead."

Twenty minutes later, Paul Mazzola watched the water rinse the bits of rice and chicken off his daughter's plate, revealing a small wooden house with an apple tree, then a car, then a small, running dog with a red tongue. "At five percent down, I figure we'd be looking at six, six-fifty a month," he said, scrubbing the plate with a soapy brush. "That new line of fly-fishing stuff has been doin' pretty well. I figure if I take in a bit of overtime, we could do that."

"You think we can make the down payment?" said Alice, returning salad dressing and ketchup and leftovers to the refrigerator. "Where's Tommy?"

"On the veranda, I think." Paul Mazzola looked through the small wooden window connecting the kitchen to the cabin's screened-in porch. "He's doing a puzzle. I think we could," he continued, after a pause. "We're almost there already."

Alice was wiping down the counter. "Let's talk to that Fiedler woman tomorrow, then. I can drop the kids off at—" Wiping the stove in small, tight circles, Alice Mazzola suddenly stopped. "Hey, Tommy," she called, and for the rest of his life, Paul Mazzola would recall the precise quality of her voice at that instant, the moment's sudden metamorphosis into nightmare. "Where's your sister?"

"She's with Chop-Chop," said Tommy.

Though the thought surged through them both at precisely the same time, Paul Mazzola, an athletic man, was three steps behind at the door. Someone was screaming something, the sound high-pitched, terrified, like an animal fighting for its life. He realized it was coming from his own mouth. Ahead of him, the door through which his wife had passed was suddenly open. Unable to breathe, the adrenaline pounding in his chest, Paul Mazzola hurtled around the edge of the cabin just in time to see his wife, fully dressed and without a moment's hesitation, arc off the end of the dock into the silent water, and before the darkness of the lake crashed up to meet him, he still had time to wonder how, without any sign or mark, she could have known.

Six feet down, reaching through the sedimented dark as surely as though following some new umbilical, Alice Mazzola's hand closed on her daughter's forearm, half buried in the soft, annealing mud. There was no time to think, no time for the heart to seize and cramp. In the next instant, it seemed, she had her daughter's small head cradled in her hands and her own mouth over hers and was breathing, breathing, pumping the palm-sized rib cage, then breathing again into that incomprehensible stillness, and Paul Mazzola, kneeling beside them, could hear himself saying, over and over again, "Oh Jesus, oh please, oh my god, please, oh god, please, give her back," and nothing happening and his wife breathing and pumping and breathing again and the darkness coming down and then suddenly the little body shuddered and vomitted up a gush of water smooth with algae and flecked with bits of rice, and as Alice Mazzola gathered up her soaking, heaving daughter in her arms, crying now, the silent spheres—unseen, unheard—adjusted, and momentarily came to balance.

the offering—
a sketch

The evening I returned to the lake after thirty years elsewhere, I went out on the canoe, dazed with memories and the babble of ghosts, and caught three bass—sleek, clean fish, vibrant with life—and put them on a metal stringer that rattled against the side like a chain being dragged up some subterranean staircase, thinking to show them off on my return.

Making my way along that familiar shore, past trees still carrying in their flesh the six or eight or tenpenny nails of my childhood swings and forts, I felt strangely lost. I'd been expecting something, I suppose, some small reciprocal recognition, but all my years spent living here, and all my memories of it since, had earned me nothing. No signal, no sign. The blackberry bushes braided like wire over the narrow water to the swamp didn't loosen at my approach, nor did the turtles, on seeing my canoe, plunge any less desperately off the blackened joints of logs. Everywhere I looked, the water stretched green and thick as soup stock, littered with the wings and legs of mayflies and moths, blown out of the greenery. Back in the thickets, beyond the edge of loosestrife, something moved heavily and was still, waiting for me to pass.

Twenty minutes later, when the landscape suddenly darkened around me, leached of color, I looked up and saw that a black cloud, rimmed with silver, had risen straight overhead. I started for home, the storm growling at my back, and halfway across the lake, turning to the strange hissing behind me, saw the squall line, ruler straight, move across the waters, obliterating first the mirrored line of swamp with its purple fringe, then the doubled, dying birch along the eastern shore, yellow in August, then the very face of the storm itself.

I arrived home late, the rainwater in the bottom of the canoe sloshing up my legs with each stroke of the paddle, and walked up through the dripping woods to the cottage. I left the three bass on their stringer, fanning quietly beneath the surface, the dark-olive line of their backs clearly visible under the calm beneath the shoreline trees. After dinner, the time I'd planned to take the children down to see my catch, the rain started up again and we sat on the screened-in porch listening to it and to the sound of the geese coming in low over the trees, and it wasn't until the kids were asleep and we'd climbed into bed that I remembered them there, and picking up a flashlight, walked naked through the dark to the dock beneath the trees. I could see even before I pulled up the stringer that he was dead, the whiteness of his belly shining up through the dark (this the big one, the three-pounder that had smashed my lure by a fallen tree, then leaped once, twice, high into the humid air as though hoping to escape to some other, kinder medium), but it wasn't until I'd hauled the chain so strangely light onto the wood that I saw the marbled, staring eyes, the severed body trailing innards, the pink-white meat exposed along the back. A huge bite from underneath, deep into the gill plates, had nearly cut him off the stringer's links—he hung in the flashlight's beam by a few small bones and a pearly strip of flesh—and suddenly quite cold I released the other two, unharmed, then took what was left of him off the chain and threw it far over the water.

It sank into the dark, my penance, my unintended offering, and the moon, bobbing in an open patch of sky, wavered briefly as though touched from below and was still.